THE OTHER WOMAN

More Than Just His Mistress

Tamara Wilson

The Other Woman: More Than Just His Mistress

Printed in the United States of America

First Printing

ISBN 978-1-943284-63-4 (pbk.)

ISBN 978-1-943284-15-3 (ebk)

A2Z Books Publishing Lithonia, GA 30058 www.A2ZBooksPublishing.net Manufactured in the United States of America A2Z Books Publishing has allowed this work to remain exactly as the author intended, verbatim.

Table of Contents

CHAPTER 1

THE LONER

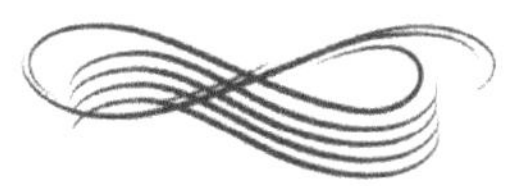

I never really had too many friends growing up. All of my school years were only dotted here and there by a few friends. Kids who were not easily bored by the shy introspective girl that I was back then. I was the quiet kind who never really went out much. My room was my refuge. The walls covered by the models I loved were the canvas upon which I first drew my dreams. Mills and boons were the foundations of the countless castles I built in the air in the endless moments I spent alone.

My silence worried my mom, so she tried to get me to go out more. However, nothing she did worked. Ensuring that no cable was ever put in my room didn't work and arranging play dates with the few school friends I had, and the kids in the neighborhood didn't work either. Somehow it was her fault. I started out my life with lots of *no's* from her. She was a *No* mom, and that affected me badly. You can't just turn a latchkey child into an outgoing one with the flicking of a few buttons. By age ten, I had become a kid who never asked for things because she was sure her request would be declined.

Being around people was something I hated. That was probably because at home I was always in a shell, my room. I was never around a lot of people. I am the middle child. I have two brothers, but we are not close. That connection that people say is supposed to exist between siblings is alien to us. Today I can't even remember the last time we bonded. I think it is a result of the lack of closeness between us all that I got used to not talking and being alone. I guess this is why I ended up being a quiet kid. Today I still blame my parents for that. I think if they had not kept me so tied up, I wouldn't have turned out to be that way.

I guess watching my parents' marriage fall apart didn't help matters either. My mom stepped out of their marriage a couple of times according to my dad. He had a big heart, so he forgave her each time she came back begging. But the last time she stepped out, she got pregnant. That was the last straw for my dad. He took off the cloak of the forgiving dad, and her repeated role of the prodigal daughter ended.

My mom remarried after being pregnant with my little brother that wasn't by my father.

My mom, God bless her soul, seemed like she was the type that just had to have a man and a big house. I say this because she remarried after my dad decided not to take her back. She remarried even though she wasn't happy with my stepdad like she was with my real dad. I could kind of tell when I was younger. I'm observant enough to know what real happiness looks like, and my mom and stepdad wasn't it. The laughter that was always on her lips and in her eyes when she was with dad, faded with time. Her smiles came less frequently, and the *no's* came more frequently.

In my teenage years, I was into modeling for a while. My dad never liked to support me in modeling gigs. He would always complain, but then he would take me. He never invested any money into the modeling either, and I even had to pay for my photoshoots. But eventually I got bored with modeling and moved on.

I was never really taught anything. My dad only taught me how to drive, and that's about it. My mother never made out time to discuss sex, men, and money with me. Dad didn't talk to me about independency or anything like that. Luckily, I didn't turn out too bad. I'm not damaged or a sociopath. I have made poor choices in men, but I never gave up the cookie to easily. I wasn't that fast. Prudence is my middle name though. To this day, I barely spend money. I'm an excellent saver. I suppose this is because I am my own person. I'm not the kind to depend on anybody, not even my own dad. I've always wanted to own everything I had. Nobody taught me that. I was self-taught in that department. I was never pressured into going to college because college doesn't guarantee you a good job. Both my parents went to college, and they both had regular jobs, they had good jobs and bad jobs.

To this day, I'm still the same way; I was as a kid. Nevertheless, I am not shy like I used to be. I grew out of that. Although I'm still a bit quiet I now talk to more people than I used to. This is mostly people that I'm comfortable around. I even have a few friends now. Chief among them is Victoria, my cousin from my father's side. I know it's kind of strange to call my friend my cousin, but then, as of now, she is the only one in my life that enjoys and provides all the privileges that are meant for friends. We share secrets and try to meet up for drinks every Sunday. So, I think that's enough justification for referring to her as a friend.

CHAPTER 2

THE FIRST ENCOUNTER

This is one of those days when it's impossible to keep a smile away from my face, remove the bounce from my steps, and stop the exaggerated swinging of my hips. I woke up on the best side of the bed, whatever that side is, so I feel good about myself. It is going to be a good day. I'm completely sure of it.

My eyes are on the mirror on the wall to my right as I walk. How can I not admire the pretty lady I was staring at? Of course, I'm checking out my ass when I run into him. It felt like running into a brick wall. The impact makes me reel backward with my arms flapping as I struggle to keep myself from falling backwards on my ass. It doesn't help me because I found myself sitting on the floor, suddenly out of breathe.

"Uh-oh," the man I collided with is bending over me with a look of concern on his face. The expression on his face is that kind drivers wear when they realize they have just knocked down a pedestrian. "I'm sorry" he says putting out his hand.

After a brief moment of hesitation, I take the hand so he can pull me up. He does it effortlessly as if I am weightless.

"I'm so sorry," he says again. "Are you okay?"

I want to answer his question, but all I do is stare at him. From his looks, he is way past his youth, but still absolutely fine. His skin is that perfect blend of chocolate that can make a lady drool. His mouth is full, something to suck on for as long as forever, and his nose is perfect.

Suddenly I find myself wishing I can see his eyes. I bet it's black; there is no way it's brown. But the thing is that the shades he is wearing won't let me see.

"Are you okay?"

"A kiss will make me okay." I thought to myself

"Yeah, I guess," my voice sounds like I've been running, and I'm sure there is a smile on my face as I reply.

His own face breaks into a smile, and I get a glimpse of the most perfect set of teeth I've ever seen. Wow.

For a moment, we both stare at each other in silence. It is that moment that reality sets in. Behind him, from down the hallway, someone is approaching, a *devil-sent,* come to ruin this special moment. But I'll be damned if I just watch and do nothing.

"You are so strong," I gushed.

"I am?" he looks surprised. "I'm sorry about that."

"No," I laugh. "It's a good thing."

"But I just knocked you down."

"No, kidding."

"Sorry, I wasn't looking."

"I wasn't looking either."

Miss. Intruder from down the hall has reached us. It is Rosa from my department. She has a big smile on her face, which is puzzling because she never smiles.

"Hi Trish," she sings with a voice I never knew could sound so human. Rosa only knows how to screech, like some wild bird from the Amazon forest. But as it is with all women, she has suddenly developed the capacity to make nice produce a pleasant sound.

"Hi," I tell her and quickly dismiss her from my mind. But before I turn back, I notice her giving my Mr. Handsome a flirty side eye. This woman!

Okay, this is where I have to calm down. I'm just meeting this man for the first time, and I'm already thinking of him this way?

"Ahem…"

The clearing of his throat brings my attention back to him, and I summon my most charming smile at once.

"I am Brian Smart," he says.

"I am-"

"Trish Johnson," he completes my sentence with a big smile. "I've always known your name"

"What, how?"

"Well, today's not the first day I'm saying something to you," he says with a shrug.

"For real?"

"Yeah. You haven't… I've tried to chat you up twice, but you just walked past each time"

Are you kidding me? How can anyone in her right mind ignore this six foot tall, handsome motherfucker with his long white teeth like Morris Chestnut and the brightest smile you can find on a man for miles around? How could I have?

"God, no. I never heard you" I say throwing up my hands in self defeat. "I'm not a rude person, so I don't ignore people"

"Great. I thought so too," he says.

We laughed.

"So, third time's the charm, huh?" he says.

I don't understand. "What?"

"Third time lucky," he says again. "This is the third time we are meeting."

"Oh," I start laughing again.

Someone is coming down the hallway again. It's another female. Behind her, there is someone else. God, why did these people choose this moment to start coming in?

"So, it's third time lucky" Mr. Handsome, or rather Brian Smart, looks pleased with himself.

"Yeah, I guess."

"So..." whoa, he's backing up. "I'll be seeing you around right?"

"Yeah, I think."

"Okay then."

He is walking away without asking for my number. Seriously!

I stand there for a while, staring at his back. It's big and solid like a strong man's back should be.

What are the chances that we will be seeing each other again? I'll say they look good. Since he works in this building, there is no way we won't run into each other again. But how long that will take is something I don't know.

I can't believe I have never noticed this man despite working here for close to two years now. How is that even possible?

I shake my head in confusion and continue my walk. Again, my eyes go to the mirror as I walk past it. My ass looks good in the black skirt I'm wearing. I love the way the skirt hugs it. It will be totally impossible for any warm blooded man with a living thing between his legs to ignore — especially someone like Mr. Handsome.

From his dressing, it's easy to guess that he is a senior staff here. Already I'm wondering if he's married. I didn't notice if he had a ring on his finger. Damn. My eyes never had any chance to go there. How could they when they were captivated by his face and his physique? I wonder if he was captivated the same way by my figure. I hope he was.

CHAPTER 3

GETTING TO KNOW HIM

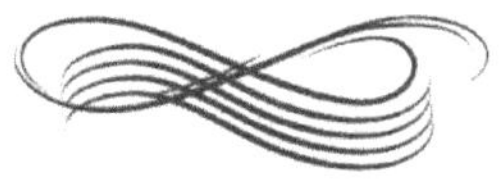

Brian is one of the coolest guys I have ever met. Any time we speak, we both usually have this Kool aid smiles on our faces. With him, it is impossible to stop smiling. He knows where the laughter is and how to bring it out from a lady's mouth.

Despite my efforts to control my eyes, anytime I see him, one of the first things I check out is his finger. I want to know if there is a ring on it. But it is impossible to find out because he always has that finger inside his pocket. I keep telling myself that it doesn't matter if he is married or not because I'm not interested in him romantically. But I know that is a lie. A fat lie actually. How can you meet that kind of man and not feel something?

The big plus about him is how nice he is, always eager to spend money on me even though I have never asked him for a dime.

As the days go by, I find that I am beginning to like him. He says that I'm his lucky charm and meeting me each morning makes his day go well.

What he doesn't know is that meeting him has become the highlight of my days as well. So, we now come to work early every morning long before opening time just so we can get to chat by the coffee machine while I get my coffee. To get deeper with him, for some time now I have been offering to buy him breakfast or lunch. But the problem is that he always turns down my offers with the excuse that he has eaten already or that he is too busy. All I want to do is treat him because he has been so nice to me.

So, since lunch has not yet become a possibility, I decided the only other way to get closer to him is by exchanging numbers. I do this in a slick manner by simply giving him my phone and asking him to put in his number so he can tell me what he wants to eat anytime he is free for lunch. He says okay with a grin and keys in the number for me.

The next day I text him asking him what he is eating. But then his response is the last thing I expect.

> *Hmmm! Well, Ms. Sweet T, I think you are a very attractive young lady, and part of me really would like to get to know you better, but the truth is…I'm married and really couldn't give you the time and the attention that you would probably want and deserve. I truly do appreciate the kindness offering to take me to breakfast. I never had someone want to do that for me. Please don't hate me for being honest, but I just want to be one hundred with you and avoid the potential problems. Thanks friend. You really do brighten my day when I see you. Love to see you smile. Please keep smiling!*

This man sent me a whole book all because I asked what he was eating? Hilarious. After pondering the meaning of his text for a while I send him a reply:

What does that have to do with me buying you breakfast?

He replies that he thought I would like to know his status.

Well, at some point I would have asked. It's not like I don't care about his status. It's just that it has nothing to do with me offering to buy him breakfast. I think he was feeling guilty about something. That is probably why he sent that letter. He knows that he is feeling me and I'm feeling him too, so he had to tell me on time. I understand.

For the rest of the day, I am kind of hurt. Even when night comes it is hard to sleep because I can't push him away from my mind.

After just two days, I realize that I really didn't have to worry too much because he sends me a text asking if we can have sex one time. At first, I am reluctant to agree. This is a married man, doing anything with him will be adultery. But then I tell him I'll think about it and he says okay, that I should keep smiling for him.

When we meet at our usual spot by the coffee machine the following morning, I ask him what he's getting me for my birthday. He is surprised because he didn't know. So, he checks my work identification to confirm if my birthday is really coming up. Then he shows me his telling me that our birthdays are back to back. This is a surprise, so I tell him that we are compatible.

CHAPTER 4

BOYFRIEND/DADDY

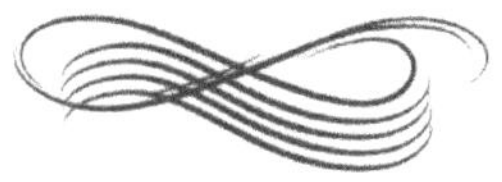

During lunch, I get a text from an unknown number. It reads:

Hey, this is daddy. This is my new number.

I'm surprised by it. So, this man has gotten a new phone all because of me, just to talk to me. I don't see how that's necessary when all we are supposed to be doing is having sex just one time. There is no need to buy a whole new phone for that. All that is needed for our rendezvous is a few text messages saying where we are going to meet and the time. After that, there shouldn't be any need for further communication on that basis. But he went ahead and got a new phone.

Now I think he has other plans and I don't know how to feel about it. On the one hand, it's cool with me. The whole sugar daddy thing is so exciting that I'm reluctant to let it be just a day thing. It supposed to go on for a while. I want to go the whole nine yards and get all of that thrill Victoria was talking about. On the other hand however, I'm thinking about his wife and the fact that maybe he just got a new phone and that's just it. However, this doesn't worry me. I'll soon find out.

My birthday dawns as one of those cold, dreary days meant for indoors. It's a good thing I don't have to go to work, or I would have felt extra cheated; another case of the company eating into my life and shortening my lifespan. LOL.

Funny enough, the first call I get is from daddy, not from any friends or family members. I've gotten used to the quiet celebrations that I do all by myself. It's a simple matter of buying a cake with some candles which I light in the dark and blow out while making a wish. I usually eat the cake alone.

Last year, Stuart had insisted on throwing a party, and I had just laughed off the idea. It was one of those annual moments of panic when he made weak attempts to get employed because he was ashamed to be an adult without a job. At that time, his birthday plans for me were based on what he expected to be paid as soon as he landed his dream job which would miraculously come a month before my birthday. I simply put his mind off it and bought my usual cake. The only difference was that he helped me blow out the candles and we ate the cake together in the dark.

This year is different however. There is daddy, and for the first time in a long time I'm actually expecting something. So, when he calls I stopped brushing my teeth and picked up the call. It's his new number that he calls from and-what do you know-he starts off with a birthday song for me. Ha-ha. His voice is not bad, so I don't mind listening and giggling as he sings. At the end he tells me happy birthday.

"Thanks, daddy" I reply. "I really appreciate it"

"The pleasure is mine Miss T," he says. "I wish you all the good things of life, baby girl. I pray that you live long and prosper…and keep glowing with that beautiful smile of yours"

"Thanks again daddy."

"You are welcome, Miss T."

"Why do you like calling me that?"

"Oh that? Same reason you call me daddy."

"And what's that reason?"

"Err…I don't know?"

I find this funny, and soon I'm laughing hard. "So, what you mean to say is that you don't know why you call me that"

"I guess so. Now can I ask why you call me, daddy?"

"Isn't it obvious?"

"The age differences?"

The toothpaste in my mouth is drying up, making me uncomfortable, but I don't mind. I just get water from the tap and rinse out my mouth thoroughly to get rid of it. When I bring the phone back to my ear, daddy is saying *hello* repeatedly, probably thinking the connection is going bad.

"I'm here," I tell him.

"What happened?"

"Sorry I went to rinse out my mouth," I explained.

"Something fly into it?"

"Ha-ha, Nah."

"Okay. So…"

"So…"

"I asked you a question."

"Oh, the age difference?"

"Yes. Is that's it?"

"No, it's not" I manage an awkward laughter as I think fast about a way to pull myself out of this situation. "You always make me laugh. You make me happy. I think it's what a super dad does for his daughter."

Daddy is laughing on the other end. His deep throaty laughter tickles me with unseen fingers. "No baby. I know what I want to be for you and it's not just your daddy"

Now I'm curious. "Okay, what's that?"

"I wanna be your boyfriend."

"You wanna be what?"

"Your boyfriend, baby."

He's laughing, and I'm laughing too.

"Yeah. We can be boyfriend and girlfriend, can't we?"

"Why not?" I agree. "That way, you can have the best of everything."

"The best of everything?"

"Both worlds."

"Both worlds…you mean…"

"A wife and a girlfriend," I explain. "Isn't that what most of you guys like?"

"Well…"

"Come on, daddy."

"I'll admit I like it too."

"Uh-huh. You are a man after all."

"Yeah"

"The dream life."

"Uh-huh. I'll take you round the world baby and get you the best of everything."

I know he's joking. At least that's what I believe. He can't be serious about wanting me as his girlfriend when he already has a wife. So, I'm playing along because the conversation is interesting. Besides, who doesn't like a bit of flirting and receiving compliments from a guy? Especially when he's as handsome as daddy.

"I'll look beautiful and sexy for you," I say.

"That's it, baby girl."

"And give you all the thrill you want to get."

"You can say that again."

More laughter follows this.

Believe it or not, our talk lasted for over three hours. At some point I beg to get off so I can go and finish up with my teeth and take a bath. He asks if he can call again, and I said yes.

Actually, I don't expect him to. But just when I finish putting on my lotion, the phone starts ringing again, and it's him. This time we go more personal, talking more about ourselves and flirting only a little bit.

I don't usually tell people about myself, but I'm so comfortable with daddy that I spill a lot. It's hard not to because he is a good listener, and he has a way of finding the positive side in all of my dark experiences.

Since I didn't get much attention from my father as a kid, daddy agrees to play the daddy role as long as he gets to combine it with the role of a boyfriend. I laugh and agree, telling him that that will make him my sugar daddy. He agrees too. But somewhere in the back of my mind, I keep reminding myself that it's all a joke.

By the time I end my discussion with daddy, I'm already late for my bartending job. I dread the kind of scowl Nick will have for me when I get in. Nick runs the bar, and he is famous for his short temper and his loud voice. Till today, I still fathom why the guys who come to the bar prefer his to the other one next door. Maybe it's because, despite the armor of anger with which he has covered himself, it is still easy to see his big heart. Men with big hearts are like big magnets. They draw other people the way a bar of magnet draws iron filings.

When I get down to the bar, I'm surprised to see Victoria on one of the tall stools. She sees me the moment I walk in and hops down from her stool screaming "She's here"

Behind her, Nick stops what he's doing behind the counter and comes out with a big smile on his face. I'm the one who's supposed to be there, not him, and I'm supposed to be getting a bad eye right about now. But what I get is his off key singing in that croaky voice of his as he begins to belt off the first lines of the happy birthday song for me.

Soon the entire bar joins in when they realize what's happening.

What the fuck?

I stand at the door, stunned. I didn't expect this. I have never had anything like this done for me. As I stand and stare at them speechlessly, Victoria comes forward and drags me to one of the tables. There is a medium sized birthday cake there with a knife stuck in it. It's a beautiful pink with a milk white icing that's done in form of drippings. Wow!

My hand goes up to my mouth.

Once they finish singing, they start urging me to cut the cake. There is no candle, but it's better than no cake, so I place my hand on the knife and cut it. This is accompanied by the cheering of the men in the bar and their girlfriends. I'm feeling good. Really good.

"Thank you all," I say, making my voice as loud as it can be. "I'm super grateful for this gesture. Nick" I turn to him and embrace him. "Thanks a lot"

"Nah," he says. "Thank that girlfriend of yours" he is pointing at Victoria. She's at the counter, cutting the cake into bite size portions.

"Vicky"

She pauses to wink at me and then continue cutting. Overcome with emotion, I run up to her and hug her from behind.

"Lest I forget," Nick says "A fine gentleman left a gift for you. I kept it outback in your spot."

"Thanks"

I accept a slice of the cake from Victoria and kiss her on the cheek.

"Thanks, honey"

"Just a few inches to the left, and that would have caught my mouth" she says.

"You are crazy," I say.

"We could do it sometime, you know"

As I pointed out earlier, Victoria is crazy. I laugh at her silly insinuations and hurry to the back. Victoria isn't a lesbian, and she knows I'm not either. But she always jokes about it. The door to the back is open, so I just push it further and walk through into the storeroom. It's stacked with liquor almost up to the ceiling. My spot is at the other end where I usually change from my work clothes into something casual whenever I get here from work. There is a small cabinet there. On top of it there is a beautiful bartending card. It reads:

> *Ms. Sweet T, Ms. Bartender, I hope you were able to do a little something for your birthday. Maybe next year we can celebrate together. Again, happy birthday, and may you be blessed with many, many more!*
>
> *Your boyfriend,*
> *Daddy.*

There are three hundred dollars inside the card. I sit on the cabinet and press the card to my chest with a smile on my face. I think this has to be my best birthday ever. There is no serious frill or elegance about it, but then it has what others never had.

CHAPTER 5

THE CAR

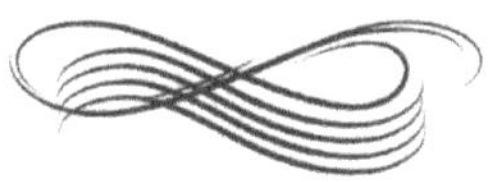

Can we meet up in my car during your lunch break today?

I'm staring at my phone screen like it's something from outer space. I can't believe that text came from daddy. Daddy, who is always evading all of my offers to buy him lunch. Daddy, who sent me a long dissertation on his marital status simply because I asked what he wanted to have for lunch.

The text is from his new number, the one he got just to communicate with me. As I read it again, I begin to think that this man may actually be serious about the boyfriend and girlfriend thing. I mean, there is no need for all of this. I don't see why he should be asking to meet me for lunch if all he's interested in is sex.

It takes a while before I reply to the text. I'm not sure if this is something I want to go into. What if it turns out that he really wants to date me? What will I do? It's wrong to date a married man, I know. But deep inside me, there is a voice that is telling me I will regret it if I allow this experience to pass me by. So, I type "*Sure daddy.*"

I imagine the expression on his face when he sees *daddy* at the end of my text. Probably a frown. He has been acting like he isn't cool with being called daddy. The thing is I don't care if he thinks it's cool or not. I'll just keep calling him that. I like the idea, and that's all that matters. So, he had better get used to it. He had better like it in fact.

Daddy surprises me when I get down to his car in the parking garage. He pulls me in for a quick hug and kisses me briefly on the lips. It's completely unexpected. I want to say something, to stop him, but I see how excited he is, so I stay quiet. There is nobody in the parking garage now, so there is nothing to be worried about.

He pulls open the door to the passenger side for me, and I slide in. There is a bounce in his step as he walks back to his side and gets in.

"I didn't expect that," I tell him.

"The kiss?"

"Mm-hmm

"I'm sorry I didn't-"

"It's okay."

"Sure?"

"It was nice."

He looks surprised. "You like it?"

"Yeah"

"But it was very short."

"Well, you can make it long."

Without another word, he kisses me again. This time he does it slowly, teasing my lips and then sucking on them gently. Okay, this is when I actually enjoy it. My last kiss was Stuart, and that was ages ago.

Daddy's eyes are shining when I look up from his lips. I wiggle my eyebrows at him, and he bursts into laughter. When he stops laughing he says "Thanks"

"For what?" I ask him.

"For the kiss. Your lips taste good."

"Yours too."

"Really?"

"Why do you think I asked for a second?"

I watch as his eyes get lit up. The compliment hit the right spot. Now he's going to start feeling extra good about himself and his kissing game.

"So, how has your day been?" I ask changing the topic.

"Great so far." He replies. "I met with my good luck charm this morning."

"Awww"

Jeez, I didn't mean to do that.

"How's your own day going?" he asks.

"Great too. Considering I just got kissed by a handsome man."

This one gets him in a tender spot. I watch as he laughs first, then stops to stare at me affectionately. "This handsome man is happy he got to kiss you today."

"Uh-huh"

"Are we going to get lunch or what?" I ask him. I haven't forgotten that this is my lunch break.

"Oh, I'm off now" he says. "But I could get you lunch"

"Thanks, daddy."

He scrunches up his face in fake anger, and I laugh at him.

"Daddy, daddy, daddy."

He better get used to it. I'm in my late twenties, and he is in his fifties. So, what better way is there to describe our budding relationship?

Today we are at Mr. Everything. Daddy's paying for my lunch, but he's with me this time. I guess I should call this our first date or outing. It's somewhat weird because we can't even sit to eat the food. Instead, we are just getting takeout and heading back to his car real fast.

Daddy says he would have loved to hang out here with me, but he doesn't have a lot of time. There is obviously a lot he has to do. I think it comes with the position he's in at work. The man works a lot. Sometimes his hours are irregular, and he's getting off when I'm going for lunch and still at work when I'm clocking out. Other times he's on the same schedule as me. Today is not my lucky day, as he still has a lot of work waiting for him.

I sit quietly, looking outside at the streets as he drives us back to the work building.

"Are you okay?" he asks.

I turn and see him looking at me with concern. He's driving at high speed and he's looking at me? Does this man want to get us killed? I nod at the road and point at my eyes. He gets the gesture and laughs before turning.

"I have yes on all sides of my head," he says.

I snicker. "Yeah, I know. I just don't see them"

"Mm-hmm"

There is a brief moment of silence before he steals a glance at me. "Look if it's because of the-"

"Chill, I'm okay" I place a palm on his left hand which is on the armrest.

"Okay. But I promise you next time we will hang out," he says.

"Cool"

It's something I would have loved. This isn't my idea of a proper outing. If he's going to be busy next time, then he shouldn't even think about it. Better to wait for the perfect time than to rush things again.

Daddy drives like the devil is after him, but I don't mind. I love the feel of the wind against my face and the danger of driving at an exciting high speed. Besides he is in a hurry to get back.

We get back to work in half the time, and when I tried to get out of the car, he stops me.

"Where are you running off to?" he asks.

"I'm not running off," I reply.

"I want to kiss you."

I lean towards him as he joins our mouths in a slow, sensual kiss. This time his tongue slides into my mouth, and I welcome it with mine. We do a little tango of the tongues while his hand moves all over my body. He starts from the nape of my neck and goes down to my shoulders and then my breasts, which he fondles through my clothes. I place my hand on his chest and trail a part down, around the buttons of his shirt to his crotch.

We are both breathing hard when we stopped. Daddy's eyes are filled with wonder as he looks at me. "I love the way you taste and the way your body feels."

I give him a wink and a luscious smile and then turn towards my door again. "I can go now right?"

"Yeah baby."

I open the door and get down, then blow him a kiss before leaving. As I walk, I make sure to swing my hips because I'm sure he's watching.

The next time we meet up in his car, he's getting off, and I'm still on the clock. I'm not even supposed to be out here, but when I thought of his lips and the feel of his hands, I couldn't stop myself from showing up when he texted me.

Now we are kissing again, and his hands are moving all over me. His kisses are gentle at first, then they get hard and demanding. His hands run up and down my arms first, gently, then the next thing they are at my breast, kneading them through my bra. I wish I can take the damn thing off, and at the same time I'm grateful I can't here. Although I'm enjoying everything, I still think it's too early.

His cellphone begins to ring. It comes to life a customized ringtone, a song I can't identify. He breaks off kissing immediately and picks it off the dashboard. When he gets a look at the screen, his eyes go wild, and he says "Shit"

"What's up?" I ask, wondering who it is.

"My wife," he says and starts up the car with shaky hands. What the hell?

I think the reason he started the car is to make it look like he's on his way out of the parking garage when he isn't. This leads me to the conclusion that his wife is the kind that monitors her spouse.

There is a forced friendliness in his voice when he finally picks the call. "Hi, honey."

He backs the car out of his space and begins to drive out of the parking lot.

"Yeah, I'm on the way…uh-huh…I'll get it."

After he ends the call, he drives up to the entrance back to the building and stops there. "I've got to head home now"

The unsaid hangs heavily in the air between us: *please get out.*

I'm confused and a little upset. We were just ramping things up, and now I'm still feeling a bit horny. I love our make out sessions, so it's understandable if I get irritated by an interruption.

I get out of the car without a word and walk away quickly. Today just got ruined.

CHAPTER 6

MY FAMILY IS ALL I HAVE

"Baby, I need you to understand why I did what I did," Daddy says. In the noise of the bar with all the guys yelling at someone on the television, it is hard to hear him clearly. I am covering my free ear with my other hand to block out the noise, but that isn't helping much.

It's been two hours since I left work, but I'm still feeling angry and hurt because of what happened in the parking garage. I don't even understand why I'm feeling that way.

"My wife is all I have" Daddy's voice comes back to me. "Her and our daughter. She's still a kid, a teenager, a kind of daddy's girl. I don't want her mother to catch me with another woman."

This pains me like a knife through the heart.

"Baby, are you there?"

I grit my teeth.

"Miss Sweet?"

I sigh. “Look, just take care of your family, okay?”

This is the first time I’m feeling jealous in this relationship, and I don’t even understand why I’m feeling that way. I honestly don’t give a fuck about his wife, because all the time I have been with him, daddy has always treated me like I am his wife. But then I care about his daughter.

“Just take care of your family, okay?” I say again.

“You don’t understand,” he says.

“I understand. Family, first right?”

He doesn’t say anything.

“Look, you are clearly not prepared to deal with having two women in your life, so I think we should stop what we are doing. Whatever it is.”

“No, I can deal with it,” he says. “This isn’t the first time.”

“This isn’t…” what’s he trying to say? “You’ve had other women besides your wife?”

“Just one,” he says. “But I never got as far with her as I’ve got with you.”

“Really?”

“Yeah”

“It still shows you can’t handle this kind of thing,” I point out.

“No, Miss Sweet”

“I think you’ll have to turn in this phone.”

“But I got it for you,” he says, “To talk with you.”

“Yeah. But we can’t continue” I love the thrill of the whole thing, but I don’t want to be caught up in any family drama with some angry wife. “You see that, don’t you?”

For a while, there is silence on the other end.

I look around the bar with my eyes, taking in the men in the big room. They all sit with their eyes glued to the screen. For once, it seems they are all supporting the same team. From where I'm sitting on my stool behind the counter, I can't see the television, and I don't even care for it. I'm not a sports person.

"Miss Sweet, baby, don't you want to work this out?" Daddy says. His tone is pleading, and it tugs at something in me. I'm touched by how willing he is to remain with me, even though he still has a wife and a daughter to worry about.

"Okay. Let's work it out," I say.

He just better not kick me out of his car anymore, I thought to myself.

To make up for the incident with his wife, daddy took me out bowling. He says he has to get his practice in for a bowling game for his wife's job or some shit like that. I don't care. I'm not exactly in the mood for bowling, but because he is putting in so much effort to make me happy, I try to get into the game.

After the first game, I find that my mood has lightened up. Daddy is largely the reason for this. The way he keeps petting me and acting like I'm his wife is getting me mushy. We kiss after every ball that drops pins down, no matter if it is a strike or not. It even gets to the extent that we are kissing after every ball throw. The way we are so boo'd up is so romantic that I'm sure I'll always remember today with a big smile on my face.

After the game, daddy takes me to the park for a stroll; we walk hand in hand taking in the cool air and enjoying the serenity of the place. At some point I find myself wishing there is nobody else here. There are some things I want to do to him now. Things that go beyond kissing. It is a pity they cannot be done out here in the open.

When we finally sit on one of the benches, I lean against him and place my head on his shoulders. He wraps his hands around my shoulders, rubbing them gently. We sit quietly, looking at the other people in the park.

There is a mother with a kid who is trying to fly a kite, and there is a group of noisy guys who are standing around a tree with drinks in their hands, laughing at something on the phone one of them is holding. A few feet away from where they are standing, a boy and a girl are on the grass. The boy is sitting with his back against a tree while the girl is lying on a blanket with her head on his thighs. They remind me of us.

"I'm always happy whenever I'm with you," daddy says suddenly.

"Me too," I tell him. "Thanks for today"

"Anything for you, baby."

I'm glad I decided to give this thing a chance.

"This is just the beginning," he says. "I'll give you a good time, don't you worry."

He's giving me a good time already.

"I'll take good care of you, Miss Sweet," He promises. "You know why?"

"Why's that?" I ask him.

"Because I'm a real man," he says. "I'm not like those knuckleheads out there"

I look up and see that he means the laughing guys. They have stopped laughing now, but they are still looking at the phone.

"I'll give you something you've never had," Daddy promises me.

I hope he does.

CHAPTER 7

MY PLACE OR YOURS

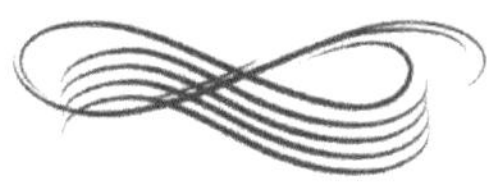

Daddy is full of surprises. Today from out of the blue, we are sitting in a leasing office trying to get a place together. He started talking about it last week, after our outing at the bowling alley. Then I thought he was just joking, but now I know he is serious.

He was like: "If I were a diabetic, you would be my insulin shots."

It was funny, so I laughed and told him, "If I were a fish, you would be my river."

He threw another one right back at me and back and forth it went, until he suddenly got serious. "You know baby, I love being with you."

"Me too daddy. You make me happy."

"I look forward to each day simply because of the possibility of seeing you."

"It's because of you that I come to work early these days."

The coffee machine is still our morning meeting place. I now take my coffee there in the morning while talking with daddy. But that is always after we share a kiss. Also, after making sure that nobody is lurking around or approaching. Then there is his car in the parking garage. Mr. Everything also comes up once in a while.

"Every time I bid you goodbye, I get sad," daddy confesses.

"I feel lonely," I tell him.

It's funny we are feeling the same way.

"I want us to spend more time," he says.

How can that be possible? His schedule is so whacked that he never has enough time. Then there is his wife, who he has to get home to as well.

"I want to enjoy some privacy with you."

Only God knows what I'll do to him if I get him alone where there can never be anyone else. For a moment, I wondered if we can just get a room in a hotel on a weekend or something. But then I didn't mention the idea.

Yesterday morning while I sipped my coffee, he said he was getting off early so we could look at some houses. He wanted us to get a place together. I was so surprised that I spat out my coffee to avoid choking. My reaction made him think that I was put off by the idea, but I swiftly reassured him that that wasn't the case. I was just surprised. That was all.

He said that all he wanted was just to be able to spend more time with me, away from prying eyes. He wanted to be able to come home to me after getting off from work, like a regular guy coming home to his girlfriend. It was so sweet I was touched.

So, when I clocked out from work, he was there in his car, waiting for me. I got in, and he drove us around town, and we looked at several places. Finally, late in the evening we found a place I liked. It was a nice two-bedroom apartment in College Park.

Now we are here in the leasing office waiting for the agent to be done with the paperwork so I can sign the paper. Daddy wants the apartment to be put in my name. He doesn't want it in his own name so that if this thing blows up, he won't get caught up in it.

On some level, it feels like I'm dreaming because the whole thing looks surreal. I mean who goes out of their way to make you happy when they are already married. Daddy is willing to risk a lot to be with me. It's a way I know that he cares for me.

None of my past boyfriends ever went this far to ensure that I had a smile on my face. But here he is waiting for me to sign.

"You can sign now ma'am" the agent pushes over a couple of documents to me, and I sign them at once. He hands me the keys to the apartment, and we get up and leave the place.

"Soon, we will be ready to move in" Daddy assures me as we go down the stairs to his car outside. In the car, before he can insert the key in the ignition, I grab him and kiss him for a long time. He is surprised by the aggressiveness of my kisses and is slow to react. But in the end, he starts to return them, trailing my urgency.

"You are a good kisser," he says when our lips part.

I don't say anything to that. Instead, I smile and lean back into my seat, satisfied.

"Um…" daddy digs out his wallet from his pocket and pulls out three hundred dollar bills. "I want you to have this."

I'm surprised. "Err…what's it for?"

"Your hair," he reaches out to touch my hair. It's getting old. I didn't expect him to notice it. "I want you to get it fixed"

"Really? Thanks", I take the money with a smile of appreciation and stuff it inside my purse. This man is really determined on outdoing himself to impress me, and he still hasn't gotten the pussy yet, and he's doing all this for me, and he hasn't gotten the ass. It's beginning to look like my happiness is more important to him than sex.

"Miss Sweet," he says.

"Yes, daddy."

He's looking at me, looking into my eyes. I meet his gaze and hold it with mine.

"I love you."

Okay, I didn't expect that. Good lord, I swear I'm blushing right now. I'm in so much shock now that I don't even know what to say.

"I just thought you should know."

His words are calm and deliberate. Still, I am unable to come up with a reply. My mind is a boiling pot of a million different emotions.

Daddy drops me off at the bar a few minutes later, and I walk in with an extra swing in my steps. Victoria will be meeting up with me here before I go home. As I walk up to the back to change, I consider telling her about daddy.

"You came in too early today," Nick hollers at me. His voice is loud and is dripping with sarcasm. It draws the attention of the guys drinking.

"Give her a break, Nick" one of them says.

"Unlike you, she has a life," another says.

Nick glares at them, but that doesn't stop them from bursting into laughter.

"I'm sorry, Nick" I say and disappear from his sight.

In the storeroom, I sit in the cabinet for a bit before I start to change clothes.

To tell Victoria about Daddy or not?

I am opposed to telling people personal details of my life. Even those close to me don't always get it. Victoria is the only other female I have ever discussed my past relationships with. I even introduced her to Stuart before we broke up. That's how much I trust her. But that's beside the point now. The problem is that she is still on my neck about Stuart. She has talked so much about making up with him that I have regretted ever telling her about his existence. You don't go and try to cuddle up to someone you rejected just because his fortunes changed overnight. Stuart is in my past now. But Victoria doesn't want to accept that fact.

I finally decide I'm not going to tell her anything about daddy.

"Are you going to sleep in there?" Nick asks from outside.

Urgh.

CHAPTER 8

FOR THE LOVE OF FAMILY

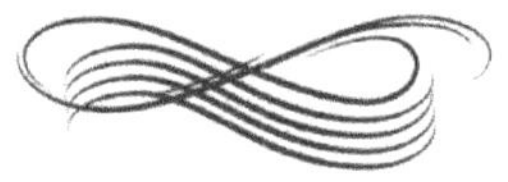

Mondays are our full chill days because we get off at the same time, so we get to hang out in his car and mess around before he goes home.

Today I'm wondering how come things haven't been super awkward between us. Usually, when people tell you they love you they expect you to tell them back and when you don't, they start to throw tantrums. When Stuart told me, he loved me for the first time I told him I was grateful for his love, ha-ha. For two days he couldn't eat. Before my very eyes he withered and began to look like some hungry refuge in a camp for persons displaced by war. I had to quickly tell him what he wanted to hear so he wouldn't die on me.

But daddy's acting so cool about it. I have a feeling he knows it will take more than telling me he loves me to get it out of my mouth. Maybe if he was younger, it would have been different. More importantly, if he wasn't already married, maybe I would have reacted differently. But he has a wife and a teenage daughter in the bargain. So, I can't start talking about love no matter what.

Today we are all boo'd up at the new apartment, and he's telling me sweet things like he did the other day in the bowling alley. We got takeout from Mr. Everything before coming here, and he insisted on feeding me the whole time, like my hands are too delicate to be used or something. We are on the couch, cuddling with his lips got so close to my right ear that his breath tickles it as he whispers countless compliments to me. Then his phone rings and he gets all panicky. I can tell immediately that it's his wife. In the blink of an eye he gets up and leaves the apartment. Next thing I know, he's out in the street. Where the hell is he going?

Why does he always have to be on the move while on the phone with her? I think she has a tracker on his ass or something. It is possible she put a tracker on his phone. What kind of woman puts a tracker on her husband's phone? The answer is as obvious as daylight, the jealous kind of woman. And that's the woman whose husband I'm getting romantically involved with. Sweet Jesus Help me.

While he is out on the phone talking to her, I try to keep myself busy with a book, but it is impossible. All I do is keep staring at the clock, checking the time, and calculating how much time he's spent outside, trying to figure out where he might be heading to within that time. It's annoying on some level.

Usually, by this time, I am at Nick's bar, but I quit last week. Nick's allowed his temper to get way out of line simply because I came in late and still hung out with Vicky in the late hours, instead of helping to clean up.

He unleashed a foul mouthed rant on me and cursed my ass out. Vicky did what little she could for me with her slick ass mouth, but she wasn't a match for Nick. When I told daddy about it, he advised me to stop working there. He could cover the expenses the pay from the bar helped me to cover. So, I quit. I know the guys at the bar will miss me. But I won't miss them much.

It's two hours later that daddy gets back to the apartment. I'm busy on Facebook reading and scrolling through timelines and low key fighting the urge to go to Stuart's when he walks in. He has a key, so there is no need for him to knock.

"I'm so sorry I had to bail like that," he says.

I ignore him pointedly and concentrate on my phone. After standing for a while and realizing he isn't going to get any word out of me, he walks up to where I am seated on the couch and squats on the floor before me.

"I don't think I'll be able to continue with this," he says.

Whoa. That one definitely gets my attention. I stop what I am doing and take a look at him. "What?"

"My wife-"

"The other day, you were talking about how you wanted to make it work, asking me if I didn't want to stay and work it out."

"I know, I know," his hands are up in the air.

"Now, here you are talking shit about everything. You can't even take a fucking stand"

I don't know why, but I'm really upset now. Pissed off. Earlier, when we had the first episode with his wife, I was hurt, but still ready to end things and make a clean break. By now I would have put him out of my mind, but what did he do? He clung on. Now it will be harder.

"I know what I said," Daddy says. "But then I can't risk losing my wife and daughter"

"You know what?" I say. "It's okay."

I get up from the sofa and walk to the window, eager to put some distance between us. I don't want him to see my face, so he won't know how much this is affecting me.

"Look, I'll still support you on the apartment and whatever you need," he says.

What's that supposed to mean? How is that even supposed to work? Are there sugar daddies who supply the money without getting the sugar?

"Are you going to turn in your side phone?" I ask him.

"Yes" he says.

"Why?"

"Because you are upset with me."

"Brian, come on" I say. "I had every right to get a little caught up in my feelings."

"I guess so."

I turn to look at him and see him standing with his hands in his pockets. "You know I didn't mean what I said"

"Baby," he walks up to where I'm standing and takes both my hands in his. "I don't think you know how important you are to me. You are more than just a side chick to me. I treat you the same way I treat my wife"

"Really?" I'm somewhat skeptical because he just went ghost on me a few hours ago just because she called.

"You are not just something to do when I'm bored," he says. "You are more than that.

Here we go again. Soon someone will start talking about staying to work things out. I don't want him to get caught honestly because I know that will end everything we have going on. And the thing is that I don't want it all to end anytime soon. Without really knowing it, I guess I have gotten too used to all of this. I will need some time to get it out of my system.

Daddy is a good man, too good for me to let him slip through my hands just like that. He hasn't even gotten the pussy yet, and he worries about me like I'm a fresh, delicate egg he has to keep from cracking. He hasn't gotten the ass, and he's breaking bread, buying gifts, paying my bills, and all of that. Who's getting played? Not me. Look at what I'm getting out of this.

I love him for how he treats me more than what he does for me. The treatment that he is giving me is so different from any other man I've dated, and that's what I love about him.

Okay wait. I just used the L word. Oh my God.

CHAPTER 9

THE CLOSER I GET TO YOU

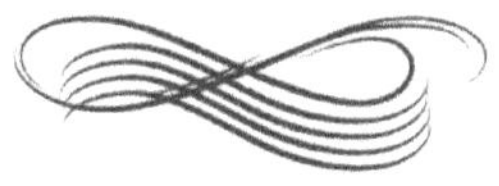

Daddy is in the apartment, waiting for me when I get back from work. The moment I step in, I smelled his cologne. The sight of his shirt and necktie lying on the couch confirms his presence. But he isn't in the living room, so I walk into the bedroom wondering if he is sleeping.

I see him lying in bed. His pants and briefs are on the armchair by the window, so I know instantly that he's naked under the sheets.

"What are you doing?" I ask.

"Take off your clothes," He says. His voice is raspy. "Come to daddy."

My heart skips a beat, and I take off my clothes without a word. I do it slowly, knowing he's watching. I want to get him so hard with anticipation because this is the first time he is seeing me naked. When I'm completely undressed, I stand for a moment so he can admire my body. I'm still young and in good shape so I can show off, let him know how good what he's having is.

"Come to daddy," he says again, and I get into the bed, right next to him. His body is so warm and so smooth and chocolate just the way I like it. I pull the covers back to see his dick, and I ask him if I can suck it. It's semi erect and feels like a living thing in my hand.

"Can I lick it?" daddy asks me in return. He means my pussy.

"Yes," I reply, but then I'm already going down on him, teasing his shaft with the tip of my tongue. I flick the tongue slowly over the mushroom-shaped head of his dick before proceeding to lick down the front to base.

Giving head is my specialty because I stayed a virgin for a long time, avoiding intercourse with most of the men who came into my life. I didn't think anyone of them was good enough to take my virginity, so I always used my mouth to suck the hell out of their dicks. But at some point, I gave my virginity away to a football star who promised me the world. In the end he turned out to be an asshole.

Daddy's dick is kind of short for a tall man, but it has some girth because it is wide and has some thickness to it. He has shaved, so I don't have to deal with any hair around his dick or on his balls. As I suck that dick, I keep my eyes on him, watching as he closes his eyes to moan a little bit.

When I begin to go faster, pumping my lips up and down his shaft, he stops me with his hand restraining the movement of my head. Then he picks me off him and turns me over. So I lay on my back and watch as he gets down to my pussy, pushing my legs wide apart. It feels so good when he gets to work with his tongue, but then, getting eaten out has never been my thing. For me, it's just an *if you want to do it type of thing.* If he loves it,

I won't stop him.

All of a sudden, daddy stops eating me out and reaches for his phone. When he looks at the screen, an odd look comes over his face, and he gets up from the bed and says he has to go.

What the fuck?

"Why?" I ask him.

"I have to go and handle something," he replies and starts putting on his briefs.

Cool. I think he's backing down again. Why is he always so damn nervous? It's not like he's the only one cheating on his wife. A lot of other men do it daily and still manage to maintain their cool.

With his pants on, he comes to bed and bends over me. "Baby, we have plenty of time to make love," He says. "I'm not going anywhere"

Relief floods me, and I nod.

"I love you," he says and leaves the room.

My heart flutters as I watch him leave. For a brief moment, I feel a mad urge to tell him I love him too. The words are on my tongue, waiting for me to open my mouth and let them fly. But I swallow them and keep quiet.

Although we didn't get the chance to go all the way, I'm still feeling good. The fact that he said he loves me again seems to have made up for everything. Besides, he also said he isn't going anywhere. So although we didn't get down to it today, there will still be other days.

CHAPTER 10

I REPRESENT HIM

I don't know why, but two days after daddy and I almost had sex in our new apartment I fall sick. I'm so sick for a week, so I didn't go to work. During this time, daddy brings me soup, fruit juices and some medicine to help me get better, and I think of how lucky I am to have him. However, it's frustrating that I can't kiss him, and he doesn't want to kiss me either. Whenever he comes or whenever he's leaving, he blows me air kisses or pecks me on the forehead if I try to hug him. This is frustrating and makes me feel miserable.

The day I get well enough to get out of the house, daddy gives me money to get my hair fixed, saying that I represent him, and so I need to look good always. This is funny because we are a secret. Nobody is supposed to know we are dating. So how do you represent someone no one knows you are supposed to be representing anyway? Ha-ha.

Daddy does his best to make up for all the time I was sick, pampering, and spoiling me as much as he can. He takes me out so we can eat and get some chicken. Although it's just fast food that we go to, it doesn't take the romance away from it all. I don't care where we go to, whether it's a fancy restaurant or a fast food restaurant, as long as I'm there with daddy, I am okay.

All through our time there, he tells me anecdotes from his college days and his high school days that are so funny that I laugh until I have tears in my eyes.

Mondays are our full chill days. They are the day's daddy can make out time to hang out with me. As a result, it is now my most cherished day of the week. I look forward to it with much anticipation.

Unfortunately, however, this Monday, daddy has to take his daughter to her cheerleading practice. But then, because he knows how important today is he's getting off earlier so he can scoop me up real quick before he picks up his daughter. Daddy is a dedicated lover. He has his hands completely full today, yet he's trying to make everything work so I won't be displeased. I kind of feel sorry for him because of all the efforts he's making. He has been working a lot lately, saying he's trying to get his money up for us. Yet in addition to that, he is also doing his best to squeeze out time for me and his daughter.

Today the plan is to drop me off at this fancy restaurant close by and then go pick up his daughter. Once he drops her off, he'll come back to the restaurant to be with me. I'm excited, and I am looking forward to our date.

As he drives us to the restaurant, he sings along to the song playing from the radio. It is John Legend's Tonight. Daddy has a fairly nice voice and the way he sings the song makes me remember the night we had sex. It makes me imagine us doing it again. Somehow, I'm tempted to make him want me tonight, but I don't. Instead, I sing along with him, wriggling my body as much as the seat belt tying me to the passenger seat will allow me.

There is not much traffic because it is not yet rush hour, so for long stretches, there are no cars ahead of us. I guess this is what makes daddy get lax. He is driving at high speed with only one hand holding the steering wheel and the other hanging in the air so he can snap the thumb and forefinger together in tune with the song. That is why when we get to the intersection, and a dog runs out into the road, he swerves too hard to avoid it.

What do you know? Next thing he's grappling with the steering wheel because the car is skidding out of control. My heart flies into my mouth as the car begins to fishtail. We end up getting bashed by another car also trying to get by and come to a sudden stop at the curb. I have a scream in my throat and by the end of everything I wonder how I managed to keep from letting it out.

"Damn damn damn," daddy says. It's the first time I'm hearing him curse, and I understand because he is probably upset about his car.

God, I'm so nervous right now. This is the first time I'm in an accident. But at least I don't have any scratches on my body; Thank God. My heart is pounding because I know I shouldn't be here with him. But the problem is that he can't drive the car this way anymore. But I can't stay here. I don't want those who know him to see us together in the car. What is he even going to tell his wife?

As daddy gets down from the car to check the damages, I whip out my phone and dial Victoria's number. The good thing about Victoria is that even if she is half-way around the world, once she gets a distress call from me, she will leave everything and come get me.

"Hey baby," she says once the call gets connected.

"Vicky, you are not busy, are you?" I ask.

"Baby, you know I'm busy all the time," she replies.

"What are you doing?"

"Breathing?"

As stupid as that answer sounds, it gives me relief. It means, of course, she is free.

"Can you come and get me?" I ask her. "I was in an accident."

"Oh my God. Baby, are you okay?"

"I wasn't hurt" I assured her.

"Okay, just give me the address, I'll be there right away."

I look at the closest road sign, pulled up my GPS and give her the address, and then I hung up...

Daddy is looking at me through the window. There is relief on his face. I think he's happy I called someone to come get me. Maybe he's been worried about how to get me back home.

"You called someone," he says.

"Yeah," I tell him. "You got someone to call?"

"My wife."

"Oh"

Of all people.

"But I'll wait a minute before calling her. So your person can get here before her"

"Okay"

"You are not hurt, are you?" he asks.

"No, I'm not," I reply and flash him a smile. "You are okay right?"

"Mm-hmm" he nods his head.

"I'm sorry about your car."

He waves away my apology like it's unnecessary. "Don't worry about it, I have insurance."

When Victoria picks me up, she bombards me with a million questions just as I expected. Her Toyota Hatchback is already a small car. But then the way she jumps me once we get in makes it feel even smaller.

At first, her questions are all motherly.

"We are going to the hospital right away" She announces while putting on her seat belt. "Where did you get hurt?"

She checked me out before we got into the car and confirmed that I didn't have any injuries. But now she is beginning to fuss at me all over me again.

"I'm okay," I tell her for the umpteenth time. "You checked me outside, didn't you?"

"I did, I did," she replies, looking flustered. "But then what if I missed something?"

"You didn't."

"I may have."

"I'm telling you, you didn't."

"Okay baby, check yourself for me okay?"

"Check myself how?"

"You know what your body feels like normally." Her eyes all roving all over my body as she speaks, checking my forehead, my arms and my legs. "Let me know if there is anything out of place."

"There is nothing out of place."

"You may be having internal bleeding or something, or you could be injured under your clothes."

"Victoria, I'm not."

Daddy is coming to the car. I think he is worried she still haven't driven off. His wife will be here soon. It won't be good if I'm still here by the time she arrives.

"Victoria, please start the car."

She doesn't. Instead, she unbuckles her seat belt and reaches over to help me fasten mine. I totally forgot it.

"Don't worry?" I tell her, trying to take the strap from her hand. "I got this"

"Shush," she says, pushing away my hand.

I am forced to watch in frustration as she slowly buckles it with all the loving care in the world.

"Hi," Daddy says from her window. "Is anything wrong?"

"No, nothing's wrong," Victoria answers him sweetly. "I'm only trying to convince her to go to the hospital."

"Trish?" his smile is strained as he looks at me.

"I'm okay," I say. "I swear, I'm okay."

"She's okay," Daddy says. "Can you take her back to work? She is going to be late."

"Okay. But we still have to be sure-"

"Vicky!" I am at my wits' end.

"Okay-okay-okay" she raises her hand in surrender and fastens her seat belt.

Daddy leans away from the car as she starts it. He waves when she starts to drive away, and I wave back at him with a wide smile on my face. Victoria catches that smile and her eyes narrow. But she doesn't say anything. I sigh in relief.

However, my relief is short-lived

Daddy's car crash has even made me love him more. That poor car had to be sacrificed for us to be together. But he has never looked at it that way. He doesn't blame me for the car damage. Daddy uses a rental car now, but he still misses his old car. Yet that doesn't stop him from trying to still make out time for me. We still manage to go out later in the week for pizza and then a Tupac movie.

I swear the movies are meant for couples alone. Before meeting daddy, the last time I went out to watch a movie was with Victoria. Then the two of us were single ladies. Even though the movie had been fun and the night had ended on a happy note I had still gone to bed thinking it would have felt better if I had someone to snuggle up to during the romantic moments in the movie.

Going with daddy is everything it should be. We are all loved up at the movie theater, and I'm so invested in him that I hardly watch the movie. I feed him popcorn and coke while he watches with concentration and pinches him when he doesn't make any attempt to feed me when I place the popcorn in his laps. All in all, it is a great outing.

On Father's Day, I buy daddy some meat print underwear, muscle shirts, socks, a card and a vagina masturbator. The poor man only has sex once or twice a week with his wife, and so it is only fitting.

Today is a Monday, one of the best days of the week, but I'm totally unhappy. Daddy stood me up earlier in the day. We were supposed to hang out at Mr. Everything, but he claims he has work to do and so cannot show up. This is upsetting. If he had told me last night it would have been better, but he had to wait until I went outside to wait for him before he called to say that he wouldn't be able to show up. Daddy brings an extra element of deliciousness to every lunch I have with him. Today I missed it. I barely even ate my food, only doing my best to pick at it until I realized I could no longer bear the sight of it.

Now he is here trying to rationalize his actions. All I want is an apology and a promise to do better next time. But unfortunately, that is not what he is interested in.

"I don't think I have enough time to commit to this relationship," he says.

This is the last straw.

"Okay then," I say. "We are done"

"No, we are not pleased," daddy says.

I sigh in frustration. "What exactly do you want?"

"The fact that it's hard for me to make out time doesn't mean I don't want to be there for you," he says. "I still want to get to talk with you and take care of your bills baby. I'm not going anywhere"

This is so unexpected that my heart is melting.

"I love you," daddy says. "I can swear that you feel something for me too."

"I love you too," I say. There, it is in the open now.

"So, there is no need to stop talking or seeing each other simply because dating is not working out."

What he's saying doesn't make sense. But then I don't care about sense now. What matters is that he said he isn't going anywhere. And I said I love him too. After he said that he loves me.

CHAPTER 11

LET'S MAKE LOVE TONIGHT

Daddy is coming over this night. Since me and him are supposedly broken up, he asks if we can still make love. I tell him, no, but that isn't my real answer. He insists he still loves me and wants to be with me, but that he is stuck in his situation. I give in and change my mind and say yes that we can still make love.

He comes over with a dozen red roses and red Vitoria Secret lingerie. He is getting even more romantic by the day. I put on the lingerie while he gets undressed in the bedroom. When I come back to the room, he's impressed by what he sees and asks me to turn around. When I turn around, he smacks me on the ass. I twerk and dance a little bit while he smacks my ass. Then I get on top of him, and we start kissing each other. He slowly takes my lingerie off, kissing my neck, sucking on my nipples, licking my ear, and kissing my armpit.

Once he's got me completely naked, he starts eating my pussy. This time he gets more into it. The first time, he didn't really get all into it like that. Now he's licking my pussy so good. He rubs his bald head on my pussy, leaving pussy juice on his head. I tell him to eat my ass too, so he makes his way down there. I've never had my ass eaten before, but it feels so good to me.

Daddy gets back up and starts kissing me in a really sloppy and nasty way. I can taste my pussy and ass on his lips. I get on top of him and start kissing him softly on his neck, making sure not to give him any hickeys. But something tells me to go on, so I go all out with the kissing and licking, going down his body till I get down to my favorite place and part, sucking his dick. I suck his dick so good and sloppy. In time I get down to his balls and suck on them too. I rub his dick all over my face, making my face nasty with sloppy spit. I'm so nasty that I even go lower, past the balls and try to lick his ass a little bit. He tightens up, however, ensuring that I cannot get through.

I've never done it either, but since we are both being extremely nasty, I figured he wouldn't mind. I lick his ass a little bit and stop. I guess I'll save that moment for when I get some drinks into his system. Ha-ha.

Daddy tells me to get on it. He isn't wearing a condom, and there is no condom in the apartment, so I go raw. I get on top and slide his dick in my pussy and start to ride him. He's holding my waist and grabbing my breast as I go up and down on his shaft. Then he sits up, and I'm getting nervous wondering what he is about to do. He grabs me and is about to lift me with his dick still in my pussy, and I think he's about to do some extreme shit.

"No-no-no" I say.

"Relax," he says. "Daddy's got you."

Daddy is strong, so we do the stand and carry position for about ten minutes. I actually enjoy being in that position because it makes me feel like he's in complete control over me.

Finally, he puts me down and turns me over. Next thing he gets in from the back and starts to fuck me from behind. In this doggy style position, he fucks me harder than I've been fucked in a while. My entire body is rocking with each thrust, and I don't want it to stop.

Soon daddy changes to missionary and starts fucking me even harder and deeper. It turns out he's a veteran in that department. I tell him to call me dirty names while he's fucking me. I like to be called names while I'm having sex.

"Bitch" Daddy snaps sliding his dick in and out of my pussy. "Dirty hoe."

I don't know why, but this turns me on even more.

"Are you going to come for daddy?" he asks.

"Yes, daddy" I say. "I'll come for you."

Daddy's digging deeper inside me. He is going so deep I can feel him in my stomach.

"Bitch" he whispers. "You going to come on daddy's dick?"

"Yes!" I scream. "Yes daddy!"

He's fucking me so hard my pussy is soaking wet, and I feel my orgasm building up.

"Daddy I'm going to *come!*"

"*Come* on daddy's dick," he says to me.

Then a moment later he starts to shake, and I can tell he is about to come too. He holds me so tight our bodies seem to fuse. There is so much heat between us as daddy begins to shake more and moan louder, holding me tighter and tighter.

My orgasm hits me without warning.

"Oh daddy, I'm coming," I say in a shaky voice, coming all over his dick, making it slick with my pussy juice.

He moans even louder. It's as if he's about to come but is stuck and can't get off me.

"I love you, daddy," I say.

"I love you too, baby" he replies and ends up coming inside me.

Afterwards, he lays on top of me, leaving his dick still in my pussy. This is not the most comfortable position, but I'm too tired to do anything about it. So, we drift off to sleep in that position.

When I wake up however, I tell him to get up because it feels as if I'll sink into the bed if he remains on top of me for a long time. The bed is soaking wet with our sweat, so I change the sheets before we get into the shower together. After bathing, we get out and sleep for the rest of the night.

He wakes me up from my sleep by sliding his dick in between my butt cheeks. I get up a little bit to lay on my side. He lays on his side too and lifts my leg on top of his leg and starts fucking me from the side, getting it in one more time before he leaves.

He's kissing me on my neck, back, ears and grabbing my breasts while he is thrusting. I enjoy making love to daddy because he can be romantic, nasty, and freaky, just like me.

Again, he ends up coming inside of me. I'm like "You just don't like pulling out, huh?"

He laughs and says, "I'm sorry baby, the pussy is so good, you're so sexy, it's hard to pull out when you're so deep into it."

"It's okay," I tell him.

Afterwards, he hops in the showers so he can wash all my loving off. I cook breakfast while he is showering: pancakes, eggs, bacon, grits, and toast.

While we eat breakfast, I tell him how much I enjoyed him last night and this morning. He tells me that he enjoyed me too and that he can't wait to make love to me again.

I can't help but be sad when he finally leaves. We hug and kiss each other for a long time, exchanging all these endearments about missing each other and loving each other.

Finally, alone in the apartment, my conscience begins to prick me. He's married, and I know this. Then even in doing what we did, we didn't even use any protection. I know for a fact that he doesn't use protection with his wife, so he's sleeping with me unprotected and will also do the same with his wife. This man is taking a major risk with me.

No man is going to risk his life and has unprotected sex with someone he doesn't care about. Men love their dick and want to keep it protected. But daddy trusted me and loved me enough not to use anything. Then he came in me twice. That's another risk he's taking, but real love will make you do crazy things.

It's not impossible for a man to love two women at the same time; a man can be with two women at the same time. No man is perfect, and when I first met daddy, I told him he was perfect in my eyes, and he'd tell me that he wasn't perfect. That's around the time he was telling me about the other woman he was dealing with outside his marriage. I was like you been with another woman? He said, "I told you I wasn't perfect." Even after he told me that I still felt like daddy could do no wrong. He mentions that God wants us to love, meaning one of the reasons why he chooses to love me.

When a man marries a woman, he has to be with only that woman for the rest of his life. He can only stick his dick in one vagina for the rest of his life. He can only touch, hold, caress that one woman. He has to be around that one woman seven days a week. I can't speak for all men, but sometimes I know that shit can get boring. Daddy wants something different, and I can tell because he was so excited to have a girlfriend. Someone else to talk to, kiss, feel and love on beside his wife. Plus, I'm a younger woman in my late twenties he's in his early fifties, so he loves it.

Daddy always tells me to stay in shape by me still being young because his wife isn't in her best shape as she is older. Like I said a man can get bored being with just that one woman. So, if the opportunity comes, most men will approach it. Men love attention, especially from other women. They want to see if they still got that game to get a woman. Married and all men still want another woman's attention.

Daddy always tells me he loves me and that he wants to be with me, but he can't leave his family, his daughter. He says that he is afraid that she will just hate him. Well thinking about it may be so depending on what her mom - his wife will tell her. I've never asked him to leave his wife. Like I said before I would never tell him to leave her. Who am I to say that? Maybe he has been low key thinking about leaving her because he was caught up in love with me. He says that even when he's with her, he can't stop thinking about me. After being with the same person for years some people just lose interest, or they don't have the same spark anymore. His wife can think everything is cool but in his mind is something else.

These days he tells her lies about his whereabouts of course because he doesn't want to get caught. I sit quietly listening to him tell lies over the phone. As for me, he's never told me a lie because there is nothing to lie to me about. I know he has a wife, but still she doesn't know about me yet.

Daddy likes telling me a lot of things. He says he would have left his wife if it wasn't for his daughter. Funny thing is I have never told him to leave his wife for me. I don't mind the fact that he and his wife are together. Yet he often talks about marriage with me. But we both know that that's impossible since he's already married. But he always insists that he would marry another woman if it were allowed.

We have even talked about having a kid together. It's one of those *joking, but not really joking* discussions. It's just like in the beginning when he was telling me he wanted to be my boyfriend and I kept telling myself he was joking while also imagining how sweet it would be to have him in my life in that way. Now when he talks about loving me so much that he would like to have a son with me, I laugh it off while imagining how sweet it would be to hold a little carbon copy of him in my arms. Really, I wouldn't mind having his son, because I'd like my son to grow up to be just like him.

The baby will be our secret. The secret bond that will keep us bound for life. His wife will never know about it.

Daddy regularly sends me family emojis. He always follows them up with the promise of loving me for life. He's so romantic. I think we should just be connected for life. Just yesterday, he pulled up outside a tattoo parlor and asked if I wanted to get a matching tattoo with him. I laughed and said yes. We were already at the door when we remembered his wife. There is no way she won't see it. And once she does, she will start asking questions. We don't want that.

Although I don't give a damn about his wife, I love his relationship with his daughter. The way he gushes about her, it is easy to see why she is a daddy's girl.

"She is the most talented girl ever," he says with pride in his eyes.

"Most likely she gets that from you," I say tracing a circle on his chest. His shirt is open, and his tie is hanging on the arm of the couch as we relax together.

"I could show you videos of her if you want," he says.

I hesitate because I don't know if I should.

"You probably wouldn't be interested in such things, ha-ha."

His laughter is forced.

"No." I reach for his iPhone lying beside him on the couch. "I want to see."

Anything that is a part of daddy is important to me. I can't care about everything that's related to him, except his wife of course. The good thing though is that she doesn't faze me. I know about her, and she doesn't know about me. If anybody is supposed to fret, it's her, not me.

The video daddy shows me is one of his daughters in the gym dancing with other cheerleaders. She is so good at it that I don't know when I give a whoop of delight for one of her cool moves.

"My wife wasn't even there on that day," daddy says.

"Where was she?" I ask.

"At home. Down with one of her migraines."

"Oh"

Now I'm curious. I don't want to ask, yet I can't stop myself from asking. He is the one that brought her up after all. "What does she do?"

Daddy works twelve to fifteen hours a day. He's killing himself with so much work it looks like he's the only breadwinner of the family.

"I took her in with two kids by another man, her ex-husband," Daddy says. "It was out of pity. She used to go through hell in his hands. He was a woman beater. Abused her every day."

I was thinking to myself, okay, but that wasn't what I asked.

CHAPTER 12

STUART THE EX

I'm just getting inside the apartment when my phone begins to ring. I keep my bag on the coffee table in the living room first and check the caller ID. It's an unknown number.

"Hello," I wonder who it is.

"Your voice is still the same"

It's Stuart, my ex-boyfriend. Oh my God.

"Stuart?"

"Yeah baby, what's up?"

Oh my God.

I sit my ass on the coffee table in shock. This is the last call I expected.

"How have you been," he asks.

"Fine, okay." I say. "How are you?"

"Doing well" he says. There is pride in his voice. Where he used to complain to me about not doing okay, because his mother put him down because he asked for a small change Stuart is now telling me that he's doing good. That's great news.

"Good to hear."

"See, I'm in town," Stuart says. "I thought maybe we could maybe hang out, do some catching up, you know."

Somebody wants to show off.

"Err… I don't know" I say. "I'm kinda super busy."

The last thing I want to do now is suffer through an awkward meeting with someone who might still be hurt that I rejected him.

"Come on baby, for old times' sake, huh?"

Classical Stuart, founder of Team Never Back down. When Stuart first asked me out, I had laughed him off. Then we were just friends looking to make a mark in the world. We had met at a job interview at some firm downtown and hit it off from there. The fact that we had a similar upbringing made it easy for us to bond. But then, I only saw him as a friend. That rare male in your life, you can tell everything. Then he asked me out, and I laughed at him in his face. But he didn't stop there, He continued for a month until he wore me down and I agreed.

I know it won't be different this time. He won't stop unless I agree to meet.

"Okay-okay-okay," I say with a sigh. "I'll try and make out time."

"This evening?" the excitement in his voice is intense.

"What?"

"Let's meet up this evening."

"I can't."

"Come on, why can't you."

"I'm still at work."

"Liar. Vicky said you get off work at five, and it's 5:30."

Victoria, that bitch. I swear I'll strangle her the first chance I get.

"Come on," Stuart says. "Is that how much you've gotten tired of me?"

"Okay." Another sigh from me. "Where are we meeting?"

"Come to Mr. Everything"

"No"

My answer was quick. I can't meet him in the same place where I usually hang out with daddy.

"Why?" Stuart asks.

"Just pick another place, please."

"Okay…um, Rossetti's?"

"Alright"

"I'm waiting."

"Right now?"

"Why not?"

"Stuart, come on," I gripe. "I just got home."

"Okay, I could come to the house instead."

No. Today isn't a Monday, but who knows if daddy will get an unexpected break and decide to come and see me.

"I'll be there in thirty minutes."

On some level, it feels like I'm cheating on daddy, coming out here to meet Stuart. But that feeling is stupid, isn't it? It's not like Stuart, and I am going to have sex or something. Besides, daddy has his wife on the side, so I should be allowed to have somebody on the side. Not that I want to. I'm perfectly happy with daddy. I love the way he treats me, and I'm not about to give that up for anything.

"You are looking good," Stuart says.

It's a lame ass compliment. It's the end of the day. All I could manage to do was take bath and change clothes before coming down here. I know I'm looking tired and I need to get a new hairdo. Whenever Stuart compliments are just clues to how bad a person is looking. I don't know why he only compliments people's looks when they are not as good as they should be.

"You are looking good too," I tell him.

He's looking good. The cheeks have filled out a bit, and his skin has a certain glow to it. But other than that, Stuart is still Stuart. He is dressed in a grey t-shirt and denim and still looks as nerdy as he used to— I wonder if he still writes. Stuart used to have dreams of becoming a writer. He planned to write a bestseller that would launch him into the limelight and abundant wealth. But all his ninety-nine cent novels on amazon have never done as well as he hoped they would.

"It's been how long since we last saw each other?" he asks.

I shake my head. I can't remember. I don't want to. The last time we were together was the night I refused to marry him. I swear if he brings it up, I'm leaving this place.

"Well, the thing is, I've missed you," Stuart says.

I nod. I don't want to tell him I have missed him too because I haven't. Daddy has wiped his memory out my mind. "It hasn't been the same without you," I say. At least that's better than nothing.

He shrugs. "I don't know if you heard…"

Here we go. "Heard what?"

"I met someone."

Does he have to bring it up? "Yeah I heard. Congratulations," I offer him a fake smile.

"Yeah. Thanks"

Thankfully he doesn't go all Stuart on me. Stuart easily gets excited about things. And once he gets that way, it's hard to stop him from talking about it. He will go on and on about it until you are ready to cry.

"We are thinking of getting married," he says.

"That's nice."

"And you are getting invited. As a friend, I value very much."

No chance in hell I'm attending. But then I smile and say, "Of course."

"Great"

The waiter comes now to take our orders. Took him long enough, but I don't feel hungry.

"What will you be ordering?" Stuart asks.

"Get me a bottle of water please," I say.

"Seriously?"

"I ate late this afternoon," I tell him.

"Oh…" he turns to the waiter, "Get me the same thing."

When the waiter leaves, he turns back to me. "So, what about you?"

"What about me?" I ask.

"Have you met someone yet?" he asks.

Damn this guy.

"Yeah I have." I lie. Wait, technically, it isn't even a lie. I have actually met someone.

"Who?" Stuart actually sits up and leans forward with his hands on the table. Men can be super jealous. It's good to see that I still have a hold on him. I'm definitely going to mess a bit with his head before I leave this place.

"Oh, he's this super cool guy I met at the bar" I deliver the lie as smoothly as I can.

I don't want him to know who daddy is.

"One of those guys?" Stuart asks dismissively and leans back into his seat.

I laugh briefly and say, "No. He isn't from around here. He just happened to be around when a match he wanted to catch was going on."

"What does he do?"

"He is an executive in one of these big blue-chip companies downtown."

Now I'm wondering how high up the chain daddy is back at work.

"Oh," Stuarts says with a nod. "Nice"

I say nothing and offer him a smile instead, a wicked smile.

From then on, our conversation is artificial. When we finally get up to leave, I'm glad we are about to part ways. But then I do what I planned. Without any warning, I lean forward, over the table, and plant a kiss on Stuart's lips. It is the slow, teasing kind that makes guys dream of what may possibly follow. He is shocked and is slow to react. When I pull back from him, I notice that he has a dazed look on his face. Ha-ha-ha.

I leave without another word, swinging my hips exaggeratedly. It has been a super awkward meeting, but then I want Stuart to see what he is going to be missing, what daddy is likely to be getting soon.

CHAPTER 13

HALF ON A BABY OR NOT

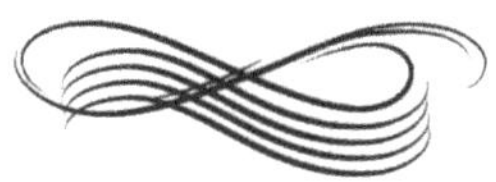

This morning started in the worst possible way. I am sitting by the window in this clinic's waiting room, waiting for my test results. I woke up this morning with severe dizziness and nausea. I called daddy and told him I wasn't feeling well. He came over after he got off from work with some soup for me. While I ate, he felt my forehead and announced that I had a fever. But ten minutes after eating the soup, I threw it all up.

So here I am in this clinic because this is getting scary. It's totally different from the first time I was sick because then, all I had was a cold. This time I can't for the life of me tell what's wrong. They have done tests for HIV, checked my breast for lumps and did a pap smear. So I'm waiting for the test results, and I'm low key worried.

"Ma'am"

It's the doctors. A short blonde woman whose looks suggest she is approaching middle age; she's come back with my tests. There is a smile on her face when I look up at her expectantly.

"You tested positive for pregnancy," she says.

The announcement hits me like a dump truck, and for a moment my mind is wiped clean. I can't think or process any thought. I just stare at her with my mouth wide open.

"Congratulations" she says.

"Thank you," the reply just tumbles out on its own. It's what you say after all when people congratulate you.

But then people only congratulate you when something good has happened. This doctor thinks that this pregnancy is good news for me. Truth be told, I don't even know what exactly it is for me.

My God. I don't even know how daddy is going to take this.

He calls just as I'm stepping into the apartment.

"How was your visit?" he asks the moment I picked up the call.

"It went well," I say.

"Okay…so what did they say?"

"I need to talk to you in person about it."

"I hope everything is fine," he says.

"Yeah. Sure"

"Okay then. I'll see you soon."

I know I won't be able to sleep well tonight. I switch off my phone immediately the call with daddy ends and go to the bathroom for a shower. The shower is a long one. I think it is the longest I have had in a long time. This is because I spend a lot of time lazing about in the bath while my mind wanders. I conjure different scenes in my mind as I try to imagine how daddy will react to the news that will make him a …well…a daddy.

In one scene, he has a big smile on his face and is hugging me, kissing me, and lifting me all at once. In another scene he has a scowl on his face as he processes the news and dwells on its consequences. I hear him asking *how the hell could you let that happen?* Then in yet another, I picture him sitting on the table with his face in his hands shaking his head and mumbling *my wife won't like this again and again.*

It takes a while to get these thoughts off my mind. Speculating wouldn't work. The best way to know what daddy's reaction would be is to tell him. That can only be done when he comes here.

I'm trying to get something down when daddy comes in. The way his tie his pulled down from his neck, I know he's coming from work. I leave my food and walk up to him for a hug and a kiss.

"Come and sit down," I say and take his briefcase from him. "How was work?"

While he settles on the couch, I put his briefcase on the coffee table.

"Work was cool," he says. "But it would have been better if you were there."

I smile. It's the whole good luck charm thingy.

"How are you feeling?" daddy asks.

"A little better."

"What's it you wanted to talk about in person."

My heart skips a beat, and I swallow hard. I wish I didn't have to tell him this now. I've tried so hard in the past few hours to guess how he will react to the news but have always come up blank. With men you never know.

"My test came back positive for pregnancy," I say. "I'm pregnant"

Daddy's mouth hangs open. Shit. He's staring at me and just nodding his head. What's going on in his mind now?

"What are we going to do?" he asks.

"Nothing right now," I say. "It's seven weeks long already"

I remember all the time we talked about having a child together, never thinking it would actually happen. Now it has happened, and I'm getting to decide if I'm going to keep the baby.

"I want to have your child," I say, surprising myself. "I want my child to grow and be just like you"

Daddy shifts on the couch so that our hips are touching. He takes my hand and asks, "Do you think you will be a good mother?"

"Yes. For our child, I'll be the best."

"Okay baby."

The original plan was to have a baby and keep it a secret, but now it's actually a reality, we have to change the plans.

"You know I'll have to tell my wife," Daddy says.

"Not yet," I tell him.

"No, not yet, of course" he agrees with me. "But eventually I'd have to. Probably when you are full term"

This makes a lot of sense. There's no way we can keep a baby a secret since we only see each other once or twice a week. Doing that would mean he would have to only see the baby once or twice a week, so he will eventually have to tell his wife so that he can have the freedom and more time to come and see the baby and me.

I know that having a baby with daddy will bring us even closer together make it possible for us to see each other even more.

"My wife," daddy says, shaking his head.

"What about her?" I ask as alarm bells peal in his head.

"She won't like this." He informs me. That information is useless. No woman likes hearing that her husband is having a child with another woman she has never met. "She will probably leave me when she finds out about this"

"You can't be sure of that," I say uncertainly. I'm thinking to myself maybe she won't but then I'm not really concerned about his marriage. My only concern is about our innocent child. You can't blame me for that. This is not about me being selfish. It is me looking out for myself and my unborn child. That is the duty of every mother.

It is hard for him to be excited about the baby because he's thinking about his wife and daughter and how this will mess up his family. This is a real life we're bringing into the world. He's been taking so many risks with me, but does he really want to take this baby risk with me? Everything is starting to hit him now. He knows he has been doing wrong all this time, but it never hit him till he got me pregnant.

"Do you not want the baby?" I ask him.

"Sweetheart, it's our baby" he says and pulls me closer to himself. "How can I not want him?"

"Him?"

"Yes, him."

Now I'm laughing. "How do you know it's a him?"

His smile is strained as he replies, "I just know, baby. I just know"

We talk for about an hour, then we kiss and say goodbye. Then he tells me he still loves me. I tell him I love him too.

Later that night, I get a text from him before I go to bed. He writes that he still loves me. But he doesn't end it with any family emoji. This leaves me upset. Where's the family emoji at now?

All through the days that follow my mood wavers. One moment I am giddy with delight because I am finally going to have a baby with daddy. I am going to be a mom. At work, it's a struggle to keep myself from daydreaming because there is usually a lot to be done, and daydreaming about my baby usually takes hours on end. It is in the apartment that I unchain my imaginations and let them roam wild.

This baby will make daddy and I closer than we've ever been. There is nothing better than a child to make a relationship stronger. I've read about that in many relationship articles. When I hit the pillows at the end of the day, no matter how tired I am, I still find myself painting our future. A bright future. It always starts with me in the chair, breastfeeding the baby and daddy lying on the bed watching us with a satisfied smile on his face.

I want the baby to be just like him. Dark and handsome and strong like his father. Of course, it has to be a boy, a boy who will grow up to be a funny ladies magnet like his father. I know he will always bring laughter to my face every day like his father does.

Unlike the nights, the mornings are hell. They come with dizziness and nausea on some days. The dizziness and nausea bring panic with them. They make me wonder if I can really go through with this. It is not like I have a choice anymore. The period in which I could have done anything about the baby is far gone. So now all I can do is carry him to full term and pop him into the world. A world in which his father is married to another woman who is not his mother and his siblings are the children of this mother who is sure to hate him and do her best to ensure he doesn't get to know them.

I know that giving birth to my baby boy will mean having more time with him, but I'm still worried about what it might do to his marriage. What if his wife actually asks for a divorce? What if he ends up hating me for ruining his marriage with my pregnancy? But then it wasn't my fault that I got pregnant, was it? I didn't force him to cum while he was still inside me. He did so himself.

Some days daddy acts all happy and excited, telling me that he's happy he's finally going to have a baby with the woman of his dreams. On those days, I go to bed in the night with a smile on my face, painting even brighter and more colorful pictures of our future together. His wife and what her reaction may be no longer matters on such nights.

On other days, however, daddy is distant and doesn't smile much. He looks so thoughtful that I can almost swear he is regretting everything. Sometimes, when he is like that, I just avoid him because everything I say to him will be answered with monosyllabic replies. Other times I confront him with tears in my eyes and ask him if he no longer wants the baby. He always cuddles me and tells me that I worry too much.

"I'm here for you baby," he will say. "I'll always be here"

What follows is a lot of kissing and making out. But we never go beyond that. All he does when we have calmed down is to cuddle me from behind. I'll playfully push back my butt against his crotch, and he will ask if I want it. I'll tell him yes, but all he will do is smack my butt and tell me to wait until his child is in his arms, then I can have it.

I don't know why, but it is around this time that Victoria chooses to start asking me if daddy is really my co-worker like I told her, or if he is something more to me. Since the day daddy and I had the accident in his car, and she had to pick me before his wife came around, she has been curious about him.

Her questions make things difficult because already I'm finding it difficult to hide the pregnancy from her. Now I 'm struggling with the question of whether I should tell or not. I'm not ashamed of daddy. Although he is almost twice my age and our relationship will probably be frowned on by society, I'm proud of him.

But then the problem is that what we have going on between us needs to be kept a secret for now. Maybe after I bring our baby into the world, we can gradually start letting people know what we have been up to.

"You are having a miscarriage."

The look on the doctor's face today is a stark contrast from what she had on her face when she announced my pregnancy weeks ago.

Yeah. Your shock is as good as mine. I woke up this morning with a very bad cramping and a lot of bleeding. The bleeding was so bad that I had to keep changing pads almost every two hours. So I had to come back to this clinic to meet this doctor again. And she's now saying that I'm having a miscarriage.

"I'm sorry," she says placing a hand on my shoulder.

This is all too much for me to handle. I thought my world was about to change because I was about to bring a child into this world, but it has all come crumbling down.

"Here," the doctor is handing me diaper pads to wear and a prescription for the pain. "You will need them" she says.

I nod my thanks and stand up to leave.

I think I did everything right for this pregnancy. My family doesn't have a history of miscarriages, so I'm thinking this is God's doing. He isn't on my side at this moment. He is on daddy and his wife's side probably because he knows that their marriage will end when she finds out about my pregnancy. My baby had to be sacrificed for their marriage. Meanwhile I have to suffer that loss and the pain of the miscarriage.

I'm not going to call daddy and tell him yet. I'll have to hold off on that till tomorrow because I am feeling hurt now, mentally and physically. I don't want to see him or anybody else for that matter.

It's evening when daddy comes by. He's holding flowers a teddy bear with a get well balloon on it. I sigh when I see him. I told him not to come because I'm not yet ready to see him, but he prefers to be hard headed.

"How's my favorite girl?" he asks, coming to the bed where I've been lying here all day.

"You didn't have to come," I tell him grumpily.

"I just wanted to make my baby feel better," he replies.

Me losing the baby is a wakeup call for him even though he will never say it is. I know it is. So now there is nothing to tell his wife because no baby is coming, not anymore. I guess it must be a relief for him.

Daddy came with carryout from Mr. Everything. We eat together on the bed with him, feeding me most of the time. Our relationship is still the same. I don't think anything is changing anytime soon. I feel like even though I lost the baby, the connection it created between us will remain between us.

When we are done with the food, he carries me to the living room where we cuddle on the sofa and watch some tv. My eyes are heavy already, so soon, he has to go.

"Thank you for dinner," I say.

"Anytime baby. I just want to make you feel good."

CHAPTER 14

CAUGHT UP

"So, what's up?"

Daddy isn't smiling this morning. I'm not smiling, either. I'm worried.

Last night when I tried to call him, his phone was off. Then I felt that he hadn't got the chance to pay the bill for the phone. However, I woke up this morning to a voicemail and a text from him telling me not to call the side phone no matter what. The strange thing is that the text and the voicemail are from the main phone and not from the side phone. That's worrisome.

"My wife," daddy says, rubbing his temple. His eyes are on the floor. "She found the side phone."

Oh my God. Shit. I'm shocked.

"She found the phone in my work bag," he says.

"How? Don't you normally hide it?"

"I was moving too fast" Daddy gets up from the couch and begins to pace the room, rubbing his bald head as he moves. "I had just got off the phone with you when she pulled up in the garage. She wasn't supposed to be back that soon.

He stops and turns to look at me "I'm sorry about this"

"It's okay," I say and walk to him. "What happened?"

"Well, I threw the phone into my bag quickly." He says. "I think that got her suspicious. Look, normally I hide the phone so well that even if she tears the bag up, she wouldn't be able to find it. But then with her looking at me, there was no way I could"

"You could have waited to finish our call before going in the house," I say.

"I do that. But then, what's the need when nobody's at home. I told you she wasn't supposed to be at home at that time. Only my little girl."

"So., you took the bag with the phone inside the house with you?" I say.

"No. I left it in the car."

"So how did she find it?"

"I think she came out to the garage while I was sleeping to check my car."

"This was last night?"

"No, the night before."

"Oh shit."

Obviously, the wife doesn't trust him.

"She confronted me about it yesterday."

"And what did you tell her?"

"That I found the phone at work and forgot to turn it in. I don't know if she believes it or not"

"So…"

"We can't communicate with that phone for now," he says. "We can't do any texting for now."

Okay, this isn't as bad as I thought it was. When he said the wife found out about us, I thought there had been some serious drama in the house.

Are you okay?

It takes close to sixty seconds for me to hit the send button. I'm curious that's why I'm sending this text. It's going to his main phone since the side phone has been confiscated and he told me not to try to reach him with it. It's not exactly about finding out if daddy's okay. Since he left the apartment hours ago, I've been wondering about the whole thing. What did the wife feel when she saw the phone. What went through her mind? What were her exact words when she confronted him yesterday?

Somehow, I find myself wishing I could be a fly on the wall, so I can see everything. It's exciting. I don't understand why, but I feel a sudden need to check out the competition. I want to see what his wife looks like. I want to know what kind of person she is. What does she do when she is mad? Does she only end things with threats? Or does she throw things around?

I try to imagine what will happen if she was a violent woman? What if she bashes daddy's head in out of jealousy? Or she traces me to this place and wakes me up in the morning with a loud banging on my door and a baseball bat in her hand. No, the baseball bat part is for men.

A text pops up on my screen. It's not from daddy. The number is unknown, but the moment I saw the first word, I know instantly that it's from his wife:

Bitch, stay away from my husband!

My heart skips a beat, and I close my eyes. My phone begins to ring. I guess it's her before I open my eyes. The caller ID shows it's the same unknown number. My thumb hovers above the green icon to accept calls. Then I shift it to the red icon and drag it across the screen to reject the call.

What have I gotten myself into? I shouldn't have sent that text. Daddy probably bought the side phone because his wife has access to the main phone, and yet I sent a text there.

All through the day, I can barely focus on the soap opera I'm watching because she keeps calling my phone.

When I meet daddy in the parking lot, he isn't looking too good. It's obvious he's lost a good deal of sleep. He's acting all cool as we get into his car to talk.

"Your wife was calling me all through yesterday," I say.

He nods. "Sorry about that."

I place my hand on top of his on the armrest and squeeze it to reassure him.

"I'm sorry too," I say. "For all of this"

"It isn't your fault," he says.

On some level, I feel it's my fault as much as it's his. I shouldn't have any business with a married man. I'm supposed to be focused on my own life, on advancing at work and shit. But here I am, messing up another woman's family. But I don't care about that. Daddy and I are still good. For me that's all that matters.

"She's threatening me" he says, shaking his head.

"With what?"

"Says she's gonna bring me divorce papers soon."

Okay, this isn't good.

Daddy turns in his seat to look at me. "Baby, I don't want my family to break up."

"I understand," I say. I don't want to be the reason his family is breaking up. But I don't want to lose him either.

"But then you are important to me too," he says.

That warms my heart.

"You remember what I told you?"

"About what?"

"About you being more than a side chick."

"Yeah I remember."

"It's true. I still feel the same way."

That's a big relief to me.

"It's just that I have my daughter to worry about."

My relief flies out the window. Why is he uncertain? It looks like he's trying to make a decision or something. Like he's trying to choose between me and his wife, and he's trying to get me to help him make a decision.

I say nothing. I'm not going to tell him to stay or to leave. It's all up to him.

CHAPTER 15

THE WIFE

I'm at work now, struggling with a spreadsheet that I can't make sense of when a call comes in. The call is coming from my text app number that I used to call daddy's main phone. It is his wife. How did she get my text app number from his phone? Does this woman have another tracking app on his phone?

I stare at the phone and do nothing until the phone stops ringing. Just when I return my attention to the computer screen, the phone starts ringing again. This woman is determined. I glare at the phone for a while, then I picked it up. Let's give her what she wants, maybe after that, she will learn to leave me alone.

"Why have you been rejecting my calls?"

That's not a nice way to start a conversation with someone you've never met is that?

"Who am I speaking with, please?"

"Bitch, you know who you are speaking with" Her voice is piercing. It makes me imagine her face covered with sweat as she is talking, standing on her feet, and then pacing her kitchen. I don't know why I picture her in the kitchen. But I guess that's because I think that even after discovering that their man is cheating, most women still go to the kitchen to cook a meal for him.

"Don't call me that," I tell her. "I'm not a bitch."

"Why are you fucking with my husband" she fires back immediately before the last word has even left my mouth.

"I'm not fucking with him."

"How long have you two been fucking around?"

Did she even hear what I said? I wonder what to tell her now. It will be silly to expect her to believe me if I tell her I'm not having an affair with her husband.

"When I ask you a question, answer me."

I can't reconcile this authoritative voice with the woman who was getting beaten up and abused by her ex-husband. Maybe she's taking that tone with me because I'm a fellow woman, and she knows I'm not going to giving her a backhand like her ex-husband. I can't even if I wanted to, and I know daddy doesn't hit women because he's a gentleman.

"Please tell me," the change in her tone comes as a shock. It's sudden. Going from bossy to whiny isn't something you do in a second. "How long have you been seeing my husband?"

"Four months now," I blurt out.

Okay that's a lie. I have known daddy for two years now, and we have been romantically involved for six months.

"You two have been having sex, haven't you?"

"No, we haven't."

Another lie. She smells it right away. "That's a lie."

"Look, the only thing we did was just a bit of oral," I say. Another lie. But this one is better crafted than the first one.

"Just a bit of oral," she mimics me. The bossy voice is coming back. "Where?"

"In his car."

"You gave him head?"

"Yeah a little bit."

"Can I ask you a question?" she doesn't even give me any time to say yes or no before she asks her question, "Do you think he's going to leave you for me?"

Her voice is laced with scorn, so I'm tempted to tell her he may leave her for me if I ask him to. But I don't. I tell her "No" instead.

"You can't tell me you were unaware of his marital status when you guys started doing whatever it is you've been doing."

She's really getting into it.

"I was aware he was married," I say as calmly as I could.

"And you still did stuff?"

"Yeah, I just didn't care about the ring."

"What if he leaves me? Don't you give a damn about what will become about me and our kids?"

I honestly don't. I didn't care about his marital status. I guess I'll also be indifferent if he leaves the wife. The only thing that matters to me is being with him.

"You don't care, do you?" she asks again. "Bitch"

She hangs up, and I heave a sigh of relief. It is now that I realize that I have been pressing the phone too tightly to my ear. The tension that grips me is thick enough to slice through.

I stand up casually and take a look around to see if Rosa is anywhere around. She isn't in sight. Probably in her office at the end of the hall. I sit back down and dial daddy's number. It's his main phone, and I don't care now.

It seems like he's busy because he doesn't pick up. But I dial his number again. If his wife can be tireless while calling, I too can be tireless. He picks up on the second ring.

"Yeah?"

"Your wife just called me."

"Again?"

"Yeah. I picked"

"You what?"

His voice actually goes up.

"I had to."

"Tell me you're joking," he's whispering now.

"I'm not."

For a moment, he's silent. I bet he's angry right now.

"Look, I didn't want to. But she would have continued bugging me if I didn't"

"What did you two discuss then? You told her everything, didn't you?"

"Not everything."

"Oh, you told her something, didn't you?"

"Look, what I said isn't important."

"Jesus. I can't fuck with you anymore."

"I only told her I gave you head, that's all" I gripe. "I didn't tell her everything"

"You shouldn't have told her anything at all."

"I'm sorry."

"You're sorry? How is that going to help?"

"I won't pick up her calls anymore."

"You've already given her the information she was fishing for, why will she call anymore?"

"Daddy, I'm sorry."

"You've ruined everything."

"I wasn't thinking straight."

"You are supposed to be down for me." He goes on, "You are supposed to be loyal to me and keep your mouth shut about this. But all you've done is throw me under the bus"

"I shouldn't have picked up her call."

"Damn right, you shouldn't have. The information you gave her is something she's been trying to get from me since she found out about the phone. I kept quiet about you. But now it's your turn to do the same, and you go spouting your mouth off"

"I didn't-"

Daddy hangs up on me then. He's so upset that I'm super worried. I dial his number again, but he doesn't pick. But that doesn't deter me. I keep calling him until Rosa shows up behind me from out of the blue.

"Is it too hard to focus on your work?" she asks.

Her voice startles me because I just checked for her earlier.

Before I leave work, I write a three-page letter apologizing to daddy. I deliver the letter to him personally with a remorseful look on my face.

CHAPTER 16

MAKING UP

I'm at work early and what do you know, daddy is already at the coffee machine. To my surprise, he has a smile on his face. It is not like his Morris Chestnut smile that gets to me. But it is still something.

"I read your letter," he says.

"Yeah?"

"I'm sorry I got so mad yesterday."

"It's okay," I say. "You had every right to"

He digs in his pocket and pulls out one hundred and forty dollars. "Do you want this?"

"If you want to give it to me," I say with a shrug.

Daddy gives me roughly about three to four hundred dollars a month for whatever I want to get. He loves spending money on me and often tells me that he wishes he could give me thousands instead of hundreds. But if you add it up, he has already spent over a thousand dollars on me. Besides

I'm not complaining.

"Thank you," I say when he hands me the money. "Take this," I give him a new phone. "You can talk to me on this. It works on WIFI"

I bought the phone yesterday because I can't bear being cut off from him. His wife thinks she is wise and can monitor us all the time. Well she is wrong.

"Awww." Daddy's eyes light up, "Thanks."

I hesitate before I go past him to the coffee machine to get my coffee.

"I will see you later today, right?" he asks.

"Yea, of course," I say.

He hugs me from behind and kisses my neck before walking away. This gets to me, and I find myself wishing he had held me for a longer time.

I love the feel of your lips on my neck and your hands on my waist.

I can't stop myself from taking a brief break from work to text daddy. I'm in a flirty mood today, and I'm feeling a little wild after our reconciliation this morning.

After sending the text, I turn back to work, but I find that I can't focus. Every now and then my eyes go to the screen of my phone to check if daddy has sent a text back. I keep checking until his text finally comes in.

I love the feel of your neck when I'm kissing it, but I prefer that of your lips.

This titillates me and gets me giggling.

"Who's tickling you?"

Glen's head pops up over the cubicle as he stands to take a look at me. He is the only person I really talk with here because he is funny, and he shares my views of Rosa.

"Somebody with ticklish fingers," I say.

He chuckles and sits back down, taking his head out of sight.

I turn back to my phone and type another text for daddy. *I love your lips too. But there is something else I love more…*

His reply comes in almost a minute: *what's that?*

Rosa is coming. So, I ignore the phone for the time being and focus on my work, looking as serious as I can be. She pauses right behind me and stares at my computer from behind me to be sure I'm not doing something else. There's no chance in hell I am. Not when she is behind me. Rosa can be dumb at times.

"Glad to see you are actually working Trish," she says. "That is as rare as a blood moon."

Now I'm trying to decide which smart ass comment to make for her; something laced with enough sarcasm. In the end, I decide to ignore her. The cow probably wouldn't understand my joke. I press my lips together and do my best to blank her out from my consciousness.

Finally, when she realizes that I'm not going to reply to her she straightens up and walks away. I know I'll have to wait till she makes the return patrol before I can get back to the phone. If I do so before she passes again, she may sneak back up on me.

CHAPTER 17

ENDING THINGS

You got played. He gave me the code. He never really loved you. You need to lose weight. Your tits are saggy

I'm glaring at my phone screen, reading this text from daddy's wife for the umpteenth time. It's the tenth text I'm getting from her today. She's been filling my phone with them since I met daddy this morning. It almost feels like she's trying to punish me for daring to meet him this morning.

I assume she saw my naked photos on daddy's side phone and noticed my small stomach pudge. Okay then. But I don't understand the part about my tits being saggy. It doesn't make any sense because my tits are small and perky. This woman is about 30 pounds heavier than me; she's no lite weight at all. She's a little chubby, yet she has the nerve to tell me that my tits sag and that I need to lose weight. Her tits are way bigger than mine, and they hang even lower. She is way bigger than me, I'm pretty small compared to her. She is just talking out the side of her damn neck, trying to find something wrong with me and it doesn't even make any sense. Well it does make sense because I'm younger and finer than her.

So, she is body shaming me. Well, daddy doesn't see anything wrong with my body. That is why he is fucking with me while he is still married because he feels like I am worth it. That's why he told me to stay in shape because I am still young, I'm not fifty like his wife, and I haven't lost shape like she has.

So, she's basically bragging about the basic shit she got going on with daddy. But I find that amusing because that is what she is supposed to be doing with her own husband? She is supposed to fuck him in bed. She is supposed to wear her wedding ring.

She acts as if she has never lived in an apartment, never was down, or needed help. She works a basic nine to five job with the weekends off. She acts as if she wasn't moving from apartment to apartment back in the day when it was just her and her two kids by her ex. She needs to remember daddy took her in with not one but two kids that wasn't his. Her ex was beating her and abusing her. As far as levels are concerned that doesn't even need to be brought up. If I wasn't on a certain level, then how was I able to pull an already taken man? Anything daddy did for me was done willingly; he was never forced. I was taking good care of myself before I even met daddy. He just took over, and all I had to do was save my money.

She wants to go back and forth with me so bad I know she feels so mad after getting no response from me. Never check the woman that your man is cheating on you with. Always check your husband, he's the one who stepped out, he's the one you need reasoning with. But it never happens that way, the wife always has to check the woman because they feel like its some competition there and they want to see what she is doing that the wife isn't.

Later in the day, I call daddy with the phone I got him. And tell him I want to meet him in the parking lot during lunch break. He is about to give me an excuse that he is going to be busy then, but I cut him short immediately.

"I don't care if you will be meeting the president of the United States of America during lunch break," I say "All I know is that I want to meet you, and that's final"

This is the first time I'm talking to him in this way. But it's not my fault. I'm feeling betrayed, and it's taking all of my self-control to stop myself from getting mad at him.

"What's up," he asks me.

"I want to see you."

"About what?"

"When you come down, you'll know" I reply.

He sighs and goes all quiet on me.

"What, you don't want to say anything?"

"I don't understand why you sound this way" he replies.

"I…" I hold myself from saying anything stupid. "I'm sorry. I just need to see you urgently."

"What is this about?"

There is a wariness in his tone. So, I decided to just tell him. "It's about your wife"

"My wife?"

"Yes"

"What did she do again?"

"Let's just meet, then we can talk about it."

"Okay," this is followed by another sigh. "I'll be there"

"Good"

When I get to the parking lot, daddy is already there waiting for me. He is standing with his arms folded and looking unhappy about being here now when he is probably supposed to be working in his office.

Once I walk up to where he is standing, I launch straight into the matter. "Did you give your wife the code?"

"The code?"

"Your phone's security code."

Before he responds, daddy heaves a heavy sigh. "Yes" It seems that is all he knows how to do these days.

"Why?" I ask him.

"She was threatening to do a lot of things. Threatening to smash our family pictures, threatening to tell my daughter and still get me those divorce papers. I just had to."

"I get it."

It's still annoying, though.

"I'm only trying to save the marriage for my daughter," Daddy sighs again. Jeez. I swear I'll just start crying if he does that one more time. "She's asking me so many questions, trying to see if you told her everything."

"What are you telling her?"

"Nothing"

There is a pause during which I try to think of what to say next. Things have changed between daddy and me. Our conversations are now stilted. They no longer flow freely the way they used to.

Just when I'm opening my mouth to ask him a question, his phone begins to ring. From the startled expression on his face I guess at once that it is the wife. She is the only one that is capable of changing him like that in the blink of an eye.

He raises the phone to his ear and says, "Honey."

As he talks with her, he begins to walk away from where we are standing. I remain where I am, trying my best not to scowl at him. I hate that he called her *honey* in my presence. It stings like a slap. Understand that I am not intent on coming between daddy and his wife, if I wanted to, I would have asked him to let her go so we can get married. But I have never brought that up. This is despite the fact that daddy himself has brought it up a few times, almost as if he is trying to give me a chance to convince him to leave her. But then they have a daughter together, so I'm not going to do that. But then it still pisses me off.

It is a while before daddy comes back to where I am standing.

"I'm sorry, it was my wife," he says.

"Is she still asking about us?"

He takes some time to answer, looking up at the ceiling with his hands on his waist and then rubbing his head a bit with his eyes closed. "Yes."

I am curious. "What does she want to know?"

"Stuff"

"Stuff like what? I want to know."

"She asked if you are pregnant, how long we've been together…"

"What did you tell her?"

"What do you think?" daddy's voice goes up. It's almost as if he is losing his patience. Maybe he's tired of being interrogated by two women. I don't care. So, I raise my eyebrows at him in a silent question.

"I'm sorry," he says.

I move close to him and massage his shoulders from behind. He sighs gratefully and resumes talking. "I told her you aren't pregnant. We've never had sex…just the oral. That's what you told her, right?"

"Yes," I assure him.

"Okay"

"So, which other questions did she ask?"

"A lot of them. But they don't matter, do they?" he turns to face me.

"They matter to me."

"Well, I didn't answer those ones. I deflected. So, they don't matter, do they?"

"No, they don't."

"Look," Daddy says. "I want things to go back to normal between us"

"Define normal," I tell him.

"You know, the way things were at the beginning."

I guess this should end it. I sigh and say, "Okay."

CHAPTER 18

THE THINGS THAT WERE SAID

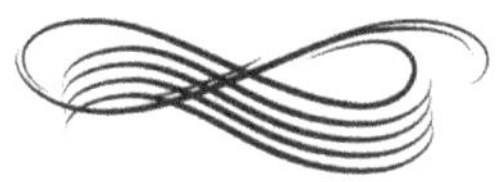

For two months, I did not talk to daddy. Anytime I pass him in the hall, he'll just stare at me, and I would ignore him. Not a word passes between us these days. That is what normal is like. Perhaps, he forgot that when he asked for normal, He didn't remember that when things were normal between us, he was the man I never even noticed even though he kept dying to speak to me for a long time. So, I have decided to make things return to that way.

I won't lie. During the time I ignore him, I miss him terribly. It is difficult walking past him in the hall and looking straight ahead like he isn't there when I know his eyes are on me, hoping I would look at him and maybe smile at him. It is hard to resist dreaming about his chocolate skin and his Morris Chestnut smile or the time we had sex or even the baby we should have had.

These days, whenever the baby enters my mind, I begin to wonder if things would have been any different if I had not lost it. I wonder if daddy would have told his wife about me. I wonder what she would have done. Would she have gone through then with her silly divorce threats knowing that that would mean paving the way for me to take her place?

Victoria is not the only friend I have. There is this co-worker of mine, Glen, who I'm kind of close to. Our closeness was nurtured by our mutual hatred for Rosa. We joke about her a lot, goofing about with caricatures of her doing silly things. Rosa is the most unpleasant person I have ever met. She is always as rude as she can be any time she has to pass along instructions to us. So, all the junior staff under her supervision, myself and Glen included, call her *the witch.*

Glen is a good listener. I guess he makes out time to listen to my tales of woe about bad days at work because I make out time to listen to his tales of misery about his girlfriend. He asks thoughtful questions and tries to make helpful suggestions. The good thing about him is that he doesn't appear to be romantically attracted to me. So, I think that if it were not for my reluctance to foster friendships with other people, we might have been besties. I think this is the reason I vented to him about the situation with daddy.

We were having lunch together during a coffee break, and he was talking about how tensed and sad I had been for the past few weeks. I tried to argue his claims and convince him that I haven't been tensed or sad, but then I found myself talking about daddy and myself. However, when I described daddy, I didn't tell Glen his name so he wouldn't know the exact person I'm talking about.

"He is this tall and dark man," I say "With the kind of smile that will melt any woman's heart"

"The handsome kind, right?" Glen asks.

"You bet," I say. "You need to see his teeth"

"Are they perfect?"

"Perfect," I affirm. "He is the type of man that will always make you laugh whenever he is around. There is never a dull moment with him."

"The dream of every lady," Glen says with a smile.

I know that is the kind of man he wishes he was. Unfortunately, he hasn't had much luck with the ladies he has met so far in his life. Although we talk easily now like old friends, Glen rarely talks with the ladies around. He is not the type that is easily at home among women. He is not like daddy. But I bet he wishes he was like him now.

"Not quite," I say.

"Well, why?"

"He's married."

"Ouch"

"Yeah. He was married when I met him"

"You knew this"

"Yeah. How could I not? It was clear from his age."

"How old?"

"I don't know exactly. I never asked. But I think early fifties maybe."

Glen opens his mouth to talk and then shuts it, giving me an odd look. When he opens the mouth again, he asks "Is it someone I know?"

"No," I replied shaking my head vigorously.

It is someone he knows. Since he works in the same building, he must know daddy. But it's not safe to let him know that it's daddy who he knows as Brian Smart.

"Okay. You know I thought it might be-"

"It's not"

My vehement denial makes him return to the conversation. "Okay. So, when you found out that he was married, what did you do?"

"I backed away," I say, wondering if that qualifies as the truth.

"Good"

"But he kept chasing me."

"Men," Glen says shaking his head.

"I won't lie to you, I enjoyed the chase, so I had no other option than to give in."

Glen chuckles a bit. "So, you two started something?"

"Uh-huh"

"Lemme guess, the wife found out."

"How did you know?"

He shrugs. "They always find out. The only thing that varies is their reaction."

"This one was mad. She threatened him with everything she could think of," I say shaking my head. "So, we had to end things"

"Uh-oh"

"Yeah. I think it's unfair, you know, every time I see him, I realize that

I'm missing him"

"It's Brian Smart, isn't it?"

Shit. My heart jumps into my mouth. God No, He knows!

"Why would you ask that?" I ask him.

"Because you are his type," he says.

"It's not him," I lie. But then I know that he knows I lied. His guess is spot on, and he knows it.

This morning, daddy is tinkering with the coffee machine when I come to get coffee. I have been getting my coffee elsewhere for over a month now. Without daddy to pay my expenses, I decided to stop buying my coffee elsewhere when I can just get it for free in here. So, for a while now I've been getting coffee from the machine.

On some days, I meet daddy there, getting coffee for himself. But I ignore him. There is always this young man with him. The man is new in our building, so I guess he is daddy's understudy, getting the hang of the place under daddy's wings. That's probably why they are often together in the morning.

To make daddy jealous, I always greet his friend while I ignore him totally. Somehow, I hope this will make him stop coming here to get coffee, but he hasn't stop. This morning, he is here again with his friend whose name I don't even know yet.

"Good morning," I greet him.

Daddy straightens up at the sound of my voice and turns to look at me. I ignore him and focus on the new guy.

"Good morning," the new guy replies. "You are looking good today, Miss..."

"Trish"

"Trish, beautiful name."

"Thanks"

I give him a coy smile.

"Look Trish, I think my friend Brian here would be happy to exchange a few words with you," he says it grandly, like the cool guy who is helping his friend get to talk to the girl he's been eyeing. He probably doesn't know we have history.

Daddy corrects that notion immediately. "John, we talk," he says.

"I have never seen you talk to her," John says with mischief twinkling in his brown eyes. "Why don't you talk to her?"

"Come on, I just told you I speak with her all the time," Daddy disputes.

"Well, I have never seen it."

"It doesn't have to be in your presence."

"Okay," John raises his hands in surrender. "Since it's never in my presence, let me take myself away to some other place so you two can talk"

He walks away, leaving just daddy and I in the nook. The first few seconds after his departure are awkward. Aware that daddy is watching me, I sashay to the machine and get my coffee. Afterward, I leave without a word feeling his eyes all over my body.

It is the next day that I finally decide to break the ice. It is obvious that daddy wants to talk. I think he is even dying to talk. So, when I see him in the hallway sipping his coffee just beside his door, I walk up to him and greet him.

"Hey"

"Hey"

There is a mixture of different emotions on his face, so I cannot read his face. So I continued by asking the general customary questions that make pleasantries what they are.

"How are your wife and daughter?" I ask him.

"They are fine I guess."

"How are things then?"

"Everybody is good, but things could be better"

He is looking wistfully at me. I guess someone is beginning to miss me, although I wonder why. Daddy is a friendly and outgoing guy, the kind that knows a lot of people. You'd always see a female at his past talking to him, or any female that passes by that do not know him. They are the ones that hug him closely every time he wants. So, I don't understand why he is still missing me. Since we stopped talking, they have seemed to increase in number. I wonder if he is trying to use them to make me jealous. All I'm afraid of another woman coming after me because of him. Especially when they see the wide grin on his face as we are talking. Okay the possibility of that happening is amusing. I can't stop myself from smiling as I think of it.

"See you around then" I finally tell daddy and sashay away. I know he's watching me from behind, but this time I make no effort to add an extra swing to my hips. I don't want him to think I'm interested in getting him back.

CHAPTER 19

CHANGE IN DADDY

It's early morning, and I'm at the room again to get coffee. Just as I expected, daddy is there too, but he's talking with Glen. When they see me coming they stop talking. I put up a nice smile for daddy when I get close enough, but he doesn't smile back. Instead he focuses on taking sips of the coffee in his hand.

"Good morning Trish," Glen says looking extremely uncomfortable.

"Good morning, Glen" I reply and make my way to get coffee.

Daddy hasn't said a word to me yet, and I wonder why. Something is not right. Just before I pick a cup I turn and greet him first.

"Good morning Brian."

He doesn't respond, instead he turns to Glen and says, "See you later." Then he walks away.

I want to ask Glen what's up with daddy, but before I can decide if I really should, he too walks away in a hurry, so I'm left confused. Daddy just gave me the cold shoulder now for no apparent reason. Now I'm wondering if Glen has snitched to him.

That will be bad. What was I even thinking when I told that guy about my private issues? Now he has gone and run his mouth. I can't think of any other reason for daddy's strange behavior this morning. This is a man that has obviously been pining for my attention for more than a month now. He never even made any effort to hide it. Yesterday when I spoke to him for the first time in a while, he got the look of a kid who had just met Santa Claus on his face. Now all of a sudden, he doesn't seem eager to talk to me anymore.

It has to be that Glen has blabbed. I shake my head and fill my Styrofoam cup with coffee. It is dark and rich as it always is. But this morning, I don't register the taste on my tongue as I drink. I'm unsettled. This is one of the reasons I detest telling people things about me. They just go off and tell other people.

I leave the room with the coffee machine feeling humiliated by the way daddy ignored me. He didn't have the right to act that way. It was him after all that asked me out in the beginning. He chased me and had an affair with me, even to the point where I got pregnant for him. This is annoying.

My mind churns with many thoughts as I walk back to my work station. In the end, when I settle down in my chair, I find myself thinking of the best way to get back at daddy for snubbing me this morning.

It is in the afternoon that a wicked idea enters my head. The moment I think of it, I smile and rub my hands in glee.

I think you need to understand that I am not a petty person by nature. The only thing is that I am petty to those who are petty to me. Daddy should have confronted me if he felt that talking to Glen about our relationship was wrong. He could have told me he didn't like it, and I probably would have apologized, and that would have been that. Besides, I never told Glen that he was the guy in question. I only described him, something I'm now inclined to admit was not wise. But then he could have denied being the guy when Glen came to him with the story. But he didn't. Instead he chose to treat me like I was trash— something he was ashamed of. This is the same man who swore that he treats me the same way he treats his wife.

Well, I'm going to get back at him for that. Let's see how he will react to this one.

I don't leave the office building after signing off. Instead, I log into Facebook and scroll to my profile, where I click on the upload picture option. Once I find myself in my gallery, I look for those couple photos we took on our outings. Funnily he was the one who suggested that we take them. That is the very thing you should never do with your mistress or your side chick. Well it is going to bite him in the ass now.

I choose the picture where he has his hand around my waist, and my head is on his shoulder. We both had wide smiles on our faces and looks as happy as newly wedded couples. This is as boo'd up as it can get. I can't stop myself from giggling when I upload the picture.

The next thing now is to tag the right people so he will see it. Tagging daddy himself is not an option. That will be too direct. I know his Facebook account. It is something I searched out on a boring day at the prodding of my curiosity. The avatar on the account isn't even a picture of himself. It is that of a bird. His cover photo is blank.

The people I tag are those co-workers of ours who are also on his friends' list. That way, he will see it sooner or later. His wife will probably see it too. I wonder what her reaction will be when she does. I bet she will have a fit when she does. Maybe she will actually smash some pictures around this time. Or finally divorce daddy. Whatever she will do, I'm sure it will leave daddy sleep deprived in the morning with heavy bags under his eyes.

Now I'm tempted to add her to the photo too, but I don't. Instead, I search up her account in daddy's profile. There is nothing much to be seen on her page. So, I don't spend much time there.

I leave the building satisfied with what I have just done. Daddy is standing by his car in the parking lot when I come out. I halt in my tracks, thinking he's waiting to confront me. But when he looks away from me and enters the car, I realize he hasn't seen the photo yet. I just posted it after all. I breathe a sigh of relief and leave for home.

CHAPTER 20

THE WIFE'S REVENGE

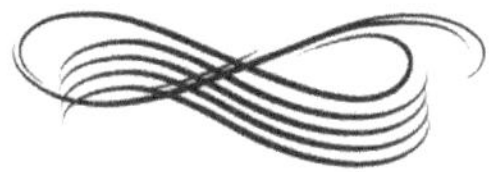

It is strange, but for a week now, nothing has happened. I have seen daddy once since I put up our picture as our avatar. We passed each other in the hallway. The moment I saw him approaching from the other end, my heart skipped a beat, and I tensed up, wondering what he was going to say. But then he just kept his face expressionless and looked straight ahead like I wasn't even there.

But that isn't what's on my mind this afternoon. I got a text this morning from management saying that my boss would like to see me today at the end of my shift. So I am on my way to his office now with a swing in my steps and a smile on my face. I think this meeting has to do with the promotion I applied for. Getting this position will mean becoming a supervisor and getting out from under the clutches of that witch Rosa. I bet she will be sad to know she won't be bossing me around anymore.

My boss, Mr. Saunders is a middle aged man with a perpetual smile on his face. It is said that the smile is always a way to put a staff at ease until he or she gets fired or gets a sharp reprimand. But I know that this morning I'm getting none of that. Sometimes his smiles bring something good.

When I enter his office, he is completely hidden from sight by his big swivel chair, which is facing the window. For a moment I doubt he is in the chair until it swings around slowly to reveal his diminutive figure.

"Good morning," the smile on his face is heartwarming as he waves me to one of the chairs in front of his desk. "Please sit"

"Thank you, sir" I settle into the comfortable chair gratefully.

"Do you know why you are here?" he asks.

Telling him *no* is similar to saying I'm not serious about this promotion. So I tell him what's on my mind. "For a supervisor position."

The smile on Mr. Saunders' face broadens, and I relax a bit. The smile is a good sign. But what follows it is not.

"Do you know Mr. Smart?"

The question is puzzling, so I ask him, "Mr. Smart?"

"Yes. Brian Smart"

Oh. What has he got to do with our meeting?

"Err…yes, I know him."

Mr. Saunders leans forward on his desk. "What is your relationship with him?"

The smile is still on his face, but now it is no longer heartwarming. It is an omen of a storm. My stomach starts to get cold, and I'm tempted to lie. But I don't. Here you don't lie. Whatever you say will always be looked into. So I just tell him the truth. He probably knows already anyway.

"We were involved at some point," I speak slowly. "But that was a long time ago. For two months now we haven't even been on speaking terms."

"Is that so?"

"Yes sir"

"Why then are you still posting photos of you two on Facebook?"

"Photos of us two?"

I posted only one!

"His wife called. She was pissed off by the photos" Mr. Saunders relaxes in his chair again, regarding me coolly. "She complained of harassment."

"Harassment?" okay, that's way off the line. "I didn't mess with anyone sir. I only posted a photo he took of us because I wanted to have it on my Facebook page"

"Really?"

"His wife is the real harasser," I'm doing my best to keep my voice from rising with emotion. The injustice of this all is choking. "She is the one who has constantly been texting and calling my phone. But I haven't even considered saying anything about it"

"Miss Johnson," the smile has finally faded his face. It has been replaced by the wintry look. The look that tells you without mincing words that you are in trouble. Shit. "We don't want you to lose your job"

My job?

I think I'm beginning to sweat now, even though the office is cold with conditioned air. Daddy's wife just hit me below the belt. If this is her way of getting back at me for posting pictures of me and daddy on Facebook, then it's way past the line. Did she have to call my job? I mean, she's trying to get me fired. Probably because this is where everything with daddy started and she knows that for the time I'll be here I'll always be meeting daddy here. She wants that to stop.

What I'm wondering now is how she got my job info. Oh, how can I forget? My one and only daddy. There is no other person that could have given it to her. But then I know that she pressured him into giving it to her. On his own, daddy wouldn't have allowed her to call my workplace. But then to keep his wife happy, he has to give her the info.

What I did on Facebook is nothing compared to this. This woman is messing with my work, my source of livelihood. It is something I cannot tolerate. Any woman can mess with my man and get away with it, but if you dare mess with my money, we are going to have an issue.

"Miss Johnson!"

Mr. Saunders' voice snaps me out of my daydream.

"Sir?"

"A penny for your thoughts."

"Sir?"

"I had to practically shout your name to get your attention."

He has a puzzled look on his face.

"I'm sorry sir."

"Look, the last thing I want, is to see you go because of some silly issue like this"

"Okay…"

Let's see what I'm getting then.

"So, you are being transferred to the other department."

"On the other side?"

"Yes, do you have anything against that?"

"No sir"

It's better than getting fired. But then it's still unfair. Totally unfair. If anyone is supposed to move it should be daddy, since his wife wants to ensure that we never see each other anymore.

"Mr. Pines will be your new supervisor," Mr. Saunders says. "I suggest you go and meet him right away because you will be starting there tomorrow"

"Okay sir."

I rise to my feet, doing my best to suppress the urge to protest against this injustice. My legs feel heavy as I walk out of the office. Once I move over to the other side, I wouldn't get to see daddy every day anymore. Funnily enough, that thought makes me feel sad. During the months I ignored him, as much as I didn't want to admit it, I still got a kick from seeing him. Seeing him every day, or at least, once a week gave me the hope that at some point things would turn around for us, and we would be back together again. I can't stay mad at daddy for too long. He is too close to my heart for that. I know it's his wife that turned him against me. He can never do anything that would hurt me. It's just that, in this case, I think he had no choice.

His wife is scared she is going to lose him to me. That is why she hit me so hard with the aim of getting me fired. She wants me to be as pissed as she is.

Now I can imagine how much that picture must have embarrassed her. Her family and friends must have all seen her husband being all romantic with another lady. She probably wouldn't want to meet any of them anytime soon because they will definitely ask her about it in the manner of friends and relations who pretend to be concerned about one's wellbeing but are in truth only curious about what's going on in her life. Maybe they would even comfort her with all the most common lies like saying that I wasn't even that beautiful, or that I didn't look smart. Ha-ha. Or they would assure her that it probably meant nothing. But then, behind her back, or behind closed doors, they would gather to laugh at her. Again ha-ha.

But it isn't really funny now.

My meeting with the boss this afternoon isn't going to look good on my employee record. This can hamper my chances of getting that promotion. Already I'm sure it has passed over me this year. The next time I can hope for that opportunity will be when there is an opening in the upper level. Even then, my chances are likely to be slim. This isn't good at all for my career.

Now I'm thinking about it, I'm feeling clear-headed. I did what I did because daddy's wife has been on my neck for a long while now. But then when you think of it, two wrongs cannot make a right.

CHAPTER 21

DADDY'S STAND

This morning I'm going to daddy's work station to confront him about yesterday. I know I'm no longer supposed to be here, but I can't let the whole thing go just go down like that without talking about it with him.

All through yesterday, I was consumed with the matter, trying to decide my next move. Would I pull up on him? I know where he lives, so perhaps a visit should do me some good. But then that will only make matters worse. I'm talking about physical assault from his wife or another call to the workplace to tell them I'm harassing her again.

The whole harassment angle is funny. It wasn't harassment when daddy was chasing me shamelessly even though he was married. It also wasn't harassment when he was eating my pussy in our house he got for us, and hitting it from the back or when I was sucking his dick and licking his asshole.

Telling me he loved me wasn't harassment, and giving me money to make my hair also wasn't harassment. Let me not even talk about the time he came inside me and got me pregnant.

Now he and his wife just messed up my reputation at my workplace. If this whole thing stops me from getting a promotion —something I'm sure is going to happen, then maybe I should file a defamation suit against daddy. It will piss him off, but I don't care. When you mess with my money, you should be ready to take whatever I give you in retaliation.

But no, I'm not taking him to court. As a matter of fact, I don't even need their promotion. I'm a businesswoman and I think I can survive without having to get paid by somebody.

Daddy is surprised to see me when I reach his cubicle. When I begin to talk to him, I keep my voice as neutral as possible.

"You and your wife tried to get me fired, huh?"

"Me?" he asks, shaking his head. "No. Why?"

"How did she get through to Mr. Saunders to talk trash about me?"

Daddy sighs and rubs his bald head. It glistens in the light of the fluorescent bulbs above us. "She threatened me again, so I had to give it to her."

"But you knew what she was going to do with it, and you didn't make any attempt to protect me?"

"Look, I did what I had to do for my daughter." Daddy shakes his head in what looks like self-pity. What the hell? "My wife is always bringing her up in our arguments, using her as a weapon against me. She knows how much I love the kid"

I understand this. "Does she know everything?"

"She knows all about you now. She knows that we went out to the movies together and that we also went out to eat a few times."

"Uh-huh. What else does she know?" I place my hands on my hip. "That's not everything she knows is it?"

I know it's not.

Daddy hesitates and asks me, "Why are you asking? You aren't going to start something with her again, are you?"

"Yes, I am." I put a frown on my face, so he will know I am dead serious.

Daddy shakes his head in disbelief. "Do you know you can lose your job for this? Are you willing to go out of your way just to lose your job?"

"Yes"

My answer shocks him. "Your wife deserves to know everything."

Since this whole thing blew up, I've been the only person paying for our sins. But so far, he's just managed to stay above everything. I don't think his wife will leave if I give her additional information, all the juicy details of our affair. But I expect that he will get a little punishment if I rile her up with it. From my point of view, I think she has been too easy on him.

She claims to know him, yet she doesn't even trust him. On second thought, I think she doesn't trust him because she knows him. That is why she is snooping around in his work bag and his phone. I don't think though that she knew he was going to cheat and lie. In the beginning I used to tell daddy that he was perfect while he kept telling me that he isn't. Now I believe him. No man is perfect.

"You are not serious," daddy says looking closely on my face, trying to read my mind.

"I am."

Without another word, he grabs me by the arm and marches me out of that place down to the lower level of the facility. All the while, I keep looking around to see if anybody noticed our exchange, if people are looking at us as we leave. But luckily, they are not.

Once we get to the lower level, he lets go of my hand, and I shift back, putting a little space between us both.

"You don't want to do that," daddy says.

Who is he to tell me what I can and can't do?

"Who is going to stop me?" I ask.

"Me," he has a blank expression on his face. "I'm going to stop you"

"Is that a threat?"

"Yes"

He puts his arm inside his suit and pulls it out with a gun. Jesus. What the fuck? Now I'm truly disgusted. All the managerial staff in our company are allowed to carry. But that doesn't mean they are free to threaten junior staff with their pieces.

"So, you are going to kill me?" I ask daddy.

He doesn't respond. Instead, he just puts back the gun and walks away.

All through that day, all I think about is daddy, how different he is. This is no longer the man I met. I don't know what happened to change him this way. The painful thing is that our relationship went as far as it did because of him. I know I could have stopped it too, but then I was enjoying the treatment he was giving me. It was too good to stop.

CHAPTER 22

UNDYING LOVE

These days I don't even know if I can call Brian Smart *daddy* anymore. He is no longer the man with the Morris Chestnut smile that made me swoon the first time we spoke. He is no longer the humorous man who is always ready to tell me funny anecdotes to make me laugh my heart out. He is no longer the man who used to tell me that he loves me.

I guess he just changed because he wasn't prepared to be with another woman. Most men, when they think of being with another woman, they only think about the pleasures that come with it. The only thing that comes to their mind in the saying that *variety is the spice of life.* The fact that they will not have to be limited to the same face, the same body every day makes them giddy with delight. So they never think of all the troubles that come with it.

When they start, they realize too late that they have to lie often, to hide things from the woman that is supposed to be the only one in their lives.

They realize too late that despite their best efforts hiding the other woman from their wives is always impossible. That is when their problems start because two women now begin to fight for their attention. They get confused and start to think *okay, maybe, I wasn't made out for this.*

Daddy always said it at the beginning that he couldn't deal with the problems that came with having a side chick. But then he was too in love to call everything off. I guess this is why I still love him to this day. The fact that he loved me so much that it was hard to let go even when it meant nearly ruining his marriage.

Funnily enough, even though I still love daddy, I also hate him. I still feel that he treated me fairly. Some days I find myself wishing there was a way I could hurt him. But then other days, I find myself wishing he was there to make me laugh and to cuddle with me at night when I lie down to sleep.

I don't know if he still thinks about me if he feels the same way about me. I'm not sure though. It's probably easy for him to lose his love for me because he already has someone else to love. All he has to do is pay more attention to her, and he will learn to forget. But I have no one else to love now. I guess that's why he comes up in my mind sometimes and I still find myself thinking about him in my moments of idleness. I don't think finding anyone like him will be easy. I have dated different men. But none of my boyfriends was on his level.

My loneliness feels like a punishment. I don't know how long it will last.

At work, our paths still cross once in a while. On days like that I want to search his eyes to see if there is still any spark in them when he sees me.

But then those damn shades are always in the way. So I just exchange greetings with him with carefully measured smiles and go my way. For now, it can't go beyond that. I know his wife is still lurking in the shadows, alert and watching closely. I can't have anybody calling Mr. Saunders again to complain of *harassment.*

But then that doesn't mean I'm going to let daddy go just like that. Despite the bad blood, I'm still reluctant to forget about him. He's too good for me to just forget about him. I just need to come up with a new plan.